I've travelled the world twice over,
Met the famous: saints and sinners,
Poets and artists, kings and queens,
Old stars and hopeful beginners,
I've been where no-one's been before,
Learned secrets from writers and cooks
All with one library ticket
To the wonderful world of books.

© JANICE JAMES.

CHRISTOPHER

The central figure in this story is a quiet, nine-year-old boy, the son of a well-known actress who shows little affection for him. At preparatory school he finds the security missing at home and begins to blossom until a near fatal accident reveals the reasons for Christopher's earlier unhappiness. Events move rapidly, until it seems that nothing will prevent tragedy overtaking not only the boy but also those most closely concerned with the care of him.

Books by Margaret Yorke
in the Ulverscroft Large Print Series:

GRAVE MATTERS
DEAD IN THE MORNING
SILENT WITNESS
CAST FOR DEATH
THE SMOOTH FACE OF EVIL
FIND ME A VILLAIN
INTIMATE KILL
SAFELY TO THE GRAVE
MORTAL REMAINS
SUMMER FLIGHT
EVIDENCE TO DESTROY
CHRISTOPHER

MARGARET YORKE

CHRISTOPHER

Complete and Unabridged

ULVERSCROFT
Leicester

First Large Print Edition
published September 1988

Copyright © 1959 by Margaret Yorke

British Library CIP Data

Yorke, Margaret
    Christopher.—Large print ed.—
    Ulverscroft large print series: mystery
    I. Title
    823′.914[F]

    ISBN 0-7089-1875-1

Published by
F. A. Thorpe (Publishing) Ltd.
Anstey, Leicestershire
Set by Rowland Phototypesetting Ltd.
Bury St. Edmunds, Suffolk
Printed and bound in Great Britain by
T. J. Press (Padstow) Ltd., Padstow, Cornwall

"But whoso shall offend one
of these little ones . . ."

ST. MATTHEW. *Chapter 18, Verse 6.*

1

CHRISTOPHER sat silently huddled in a corner of the compartment. He stared fiercely at the drab tenement buildings flashing past the windows of the train and willed no tear to fall. By much blinking at last he managed to clear his vision without more than one small sweep of his already grubby little hand across his eyes.

Peter Farquhar, touring along the corridor and into the compartments containing the boys from Arrowhurst School, did not miss the signs of distress in Christopher. He put his head round the door and had a cheery word for the other boys who rowdily boasted of their holiday exploits, but he knew that a kind word wrongly timed can undermine the most iron self-control, and so he ignored Christopher.

"Was that your mater at the station, Wilson?" asked Roberts, a tall, red-headed boy with freckles peppering his snub nose.

1

"What? Oh, yes." Christopher looked round with a start. "She—she'll be back home again by now." His voice trailed off. Roberts lost interest and produced a crumpled bag of sweets; he began to suck one, neglecting to hand them round until set upon by his companions. Christopher returned to his contemplations of the scene beyond the windows, but in his mind it was his mother that he saw.

She would be back at the flat now, going into her bedroom to throw her gay pink hat down on the bed and then making a face at herself in the mirror as he had so often seen her do, the last time only this afternoon before they left for the station. Mother had never before taken him to the train, but today there had been no one else to do it. She had nearly sent him alone in a taxi; Christopher assured her he would manage, though he was inwardly terrified of losing himself at the terminus and catching the wrong train. In the end his mother had realised something like that would certainly happen and she had come; after much grumbling she had ultimately quite enjoyed dressing herself up and stepping along the platform in her high-heeled

2

shoes to meet Mr. Farquhar. Christopher had walked importantly beside her, clutching his overnight bag, stiff with pride. Not many boys had a mother who was a famous actress. No one but he heard her say impatiently: "Oh, Christopher, for heaven's sake pull your stockings up, they're all round your ankles. Why on earth can't you keep them up like all these other boys?"

Christopher bent meekly to do as he was told. Even in their last moments together he had failed her by having descending stockings. He straightened in time to see her advance upon Mr. Farquhar with hand outstretched saying, "How do you do?" and Christopher, coming up behind, saw an admiring look upon Peter Farquhar's smooth young face as he shook hands with her and introduced himself.

"Why didn't your mater stay till the train left?" demanded Roberts now, fixing Christopher with a penetrating amber eye.

"Oh, she—she has to go out to tea," he improvised hastily.

"She looks nice," Roberts allowed.

"Yes."

"Mine always cries when I go away,"

boasted Jones II, a very small boy with tow-coloured hair hanging into his eyes.

"Mine says she's glad to get some peace," said another boy, Sparrow, with wry resignation.

"I always clean my mother's shoes every day, she'll miss me," declared Christopher defiantly. Somehow he must obliterate the memory of last night, and that awful moment that he could never completely forget.

This time he had tried so hard. He had begun the holidays by bringing her a cup of tea every morning. After the first three days he no longer expected her thanks, and concentrated all his attention on avoiding slopping some into the saucer and so earning a rebuke. Then he would creep round the room and collect the shoes that were scattered about, kicked off into corners the day before. He carried them away and cleaned them in the kitchen, rubbing and rubbing, spitting as he had seen the gardener do at Gran's, polishing hard. Then he put them outside her door very neatly, like they did at The Grand Hotel where mother and Christopher had stayed for an anxious week last summer.

Presently Mrs. Davis would arrive to cook Christopher's breakfast and take mother a tray with half a grapefruit and some coffee. She would drink a cup of very black tea herself while Christopher ate his sausage or a kipper at the kitchen table. Then she would start her unending task of cleaning; whine, whine, the sweeper went in the drawing-room, and chink, clink, as Mrs. Davis put away the bottles and carried out the dirty glasses and ashtrays from the night before. Christopher helped with the dusting. Mother would get up at about half-past eleven. Sometimes she would give Christopher half-a-crown to go for a ride on a bus. More often she would say off-handedly, "You're all right, aren't you Christopher?" and without waiting for a reply she would dash out. Christopher didn't know where she went. Mrs. Davis cooked him some lunch and left at three; sometimes mother was back, but usually she was out. When Christopher asked, timidly, about her next play, he was told sharply that she was resting. He could not know that managers had stopped offering her the parts of young girls in which she had made her name, and that she would not accept the roles offered to her of heroines nearer her real age. Once in the holidays she had appeared in a "celebrity spot" on television. That had been wonderful. Mother had been gay for a week; she took him to the Zoo the next day and to Madame Tussaud's the day after; but that was right at the beginning, before it happened.

He sighed. Outside, lowering clouds darkened the fields through which they were passing. Soon it began to rain, first a drizzle, then harder, till water streamed down the windows of the train. Christopher emptied his mind, refusing to think of the missed opportunities and little disasters that had composed his holiday. He made no attempt to join in the conversation of the other boys for he had little common experience to share with them. He knew he must simply endure until in due time school, and safety, were reached.

Peter Farquhar, returning on his rounds some time later, saw that Christopher had apparently not moved an inch of face or form during the journey.

"Five more minutes, boys," he said, standing in the open doorway of the

6

compartment. He was a tall young man, thin-faced, with dark unruly hair which, when it refused to lie down, made him look less than his twenty-seven years. "Roberts, for goodness' sake wipe your face, you've got chocolate all over it. And don't leave all those papers lying about, tidy them up before we arrive. Other people will be using the compartment after us."

"Please, sir, will there be a bus?" asked Jones II.

Peter grinned. "Are you too tired to walk from the station, Jones? Yes, there'll be a bus."

"I'd better sit in front, then, sir, please, sir, or I'll be sick. I always am in a bus," said Jones with pride.

"You'd better not be sick today," said Peter grimly. "I think you can last two miles."

"Oh, sir, he can't," declared Roberts. "Last term Mr. Fitzgibbon took him in his car specially, because he was sick all over—"

"That's enough, Roberts, I don't want to hear any more about it," said Peter firmly. "Jones, you will not be sick today."

Christopher had turned his pale face away from the window to watch this small exchange. Glancing at him, Peter knew by his blank expression that he had not followed a word.

Perched on the edge of his seat, Christopher could feel the rough upholstery prickling the back of his knees. Now the beginning-of-term feeling was coming, the familiar, frightening sensation of being completely unreal. Who was he? And what was he doing here, sitting in this train? Somehow he must manage to do all the right things—get out at the station when the others did, carry his bag, answer to his name as he climbed into the coach. Then there would be a whirling few minutes while they drove through the rain-drenched streets of Charnton, up the winding coast road that ran beside the sea to the top of the hill where Arrowhurst School stood, like a fortress, on the cliffs above the Channel.

The dream feeling would go on, Christopher knew, for several days, but after tonight it would gradually diminish. As long as he could find the right dormitory and get himself into the dining-room for tea at the proper time everything would be all right. Tomorrow the Christopher of London would have disappeared, and Wilson of Arrowhurst would have begun to materialise again.

But there hadn't been the awful thing to think about last term, or the term before. As he clambered behind Roberts' sturdy form up the steps into the bus, for an instant Christopher heard his mother's voice again, hard and excited, not her usual light, clipped way of speaking, and he stumbled. Peter, standing with a list in his hand checking off the boys' names, automatically put out a hand and helped him. Poor little blighter, he thought sympathetically; an only child and without a father, no wonder he felt homesick. He must remember to ask Matron to have a special look-out for Wilson tonight.

The coach lumbered off at last with no lost boys or baggage mislaid. The rain still fell, emptying the heavens into the grey, cold sea. Peter grimaced; what a start to the summer term. But the boys were cheerful, shouting and calling to one another; not many of them seemed to mind the return to school. Heartless little brutes, thought Peter. Their parents were now, no doubt, missing them, and anxiously wondering about them; and all the boys were concerned with was to see who could make the most noise. He glanced warily at Jones II, who was sitting across the aisle from him, behind the broad, overalled back of the driver.

"Go on, Jones, I dare you," Peter heard a voice urge. "You can have my grub ration for a whole week if you do. Go on!"

Peter leaned across to speak to Jones.

"If you are sick, Jones," he remarked mildly, "you'll get no grub ration for two weeks, and you, Roberts, will get none either for suggesting the idea." He gave both the boys what he hoped was a quelling, authoritative look, and sat back. Devils, he thought, hiding a smile; wagering sweets already. That was largely why he had become a schoolmaster—because they were such little devils and such fun. He had been at it long enough to see the results it could achieve, but not quite long enough to be certain of himself in estimating matters like the will-power of Jones II. But the gamble paid off, and, nobly pale, Jones disembarked without mishap at school.

Christopher's dormitory had windows looking out over the grassy headland across the sea. Perhaps on a fine day they would be able to see France. He stared at the leaden sky that merged with the water, so that you could not tell where one began and the other ended. A steamer ploughed her dreary course down the Channel in the distance; otherwise nothing broke the monotonous expanse of grey.

Matron came to hurry them down to tea. Christopher, still in his walking shoes because no one had remembered to pack house shoes in his overnight bag, stumbled over a badly tied lace and banged his shin. Quick tears rose to his eyes. Mother was right: how clumsy he was. It did not occur to him to think critically of her for failing to see that his case was packed properly, but only to chide himself for not tying his shoelace more firmly.

The moment passed. He was by no means the only child with an ill-packed bag. Heavy feet clumped into the dining-room and chairs scraped as the boys sat down to stoke their starving bodies.

Much later there was quiet at last. Christopher lay in his narrow bed, staring at the ceiling. Whispers and giggles came from round him, but presently they ceased too, and he knew that everyone else in the dormitory was asleep. There was a lull now, before tomorrow could disclose omissions from his trunk; Mrs. Davis had done her best, but Christopher knew his cricket shirts were too small, and other things were sure to be forgotten. He sighed; his nostrils were full of the strange yet familiar smell of school, compounded of beeswax and ink, and from beyond the windows the moist, salt, sea smell. School was queer for the first few days; there were bare form-room walls where soon maps and sketches would be pinned, empty wastepaper baskets, brand new lists on the notice board, a new place to get used to in the dining-room, and this term a new form-room too. His dormitory had not been changed, but last term he had a bed near the door, where a new "squit" now lay. Christopher remembered his own first night at Arrowhurst; he had felt bewildered by the noise, and awed at the size of the building. Now, two terms later, he knew his way about the house, but he was still confused by the din made by so many other boys.

There was a long, long time till morning. The first night always went so slowly, while thoughts poured into his brain. At last he could control them no longer and he heard those words again, mother's voice, and the low rumble of a man's in answer: mother's reply, and then the silence . . .

Christopher rolled on to his face in his bed, and at last he began to cry.

Geoffrey Frost, the headmaster of Arrowhurst School, sat in a deep leather armchair and listened to the conversation of his staff as they gathered up the threads of their acquaintance. By the end of the term most of them would be thankful to part again; but tonight, renewed, they were glad to meet once more. There were some faces missing; two young men had gone to do their National Service, and two more were here instead, boys waiting to be old enough for theirs, fresh from their public schools and anxious to seem adult in their new surroundings, but looking very little older than their charges. Geoffrey glanced at them; they would probably be good at games and discipline. He wondered whether either of them would prove to be a born teacher and leader like Peter Farquhar, now the senior master, who had begun his own school-mastering career like this. After his National Service Peter had read English at Oxford and returned at once to Arrowhurst, never contemplating any other career. Not many were like that; most found the pay inadequate, the hours long, and were only lured by the prospect of lengthy holidays and not by thought of service or guidance to a future generation.

Marion Frost, Geoffrey's wife, was pouring out coffee. The two new young masters sprang eagerly to her side to hand round the cups. She smiled at them and told them who took sugar. It was routine to her now, after twelve years, this breaking in of the new and bridging of the holiday gap into the term. She had the right word for everyone. Geoffrey watched her with affectionate admiration as she talked to the two new young men, soon putting them at ease. She had a knack he lacked for dealing with the parents, and could disentangle herself from conversation with the most persistent mother without causing offence in less time than anyone he knew. Soon, now, the telephone would ring, and she would begin the first-night session of calls from worried new boys' mothers needing reassurance, and several apologetic older mothers who still had to discover whether their children had gone to bed weeping, as they anxiously feared, or had heartlessly forgotten already the very existence of home and family. Although they had been married for twelve years Geoffrey was still uncertain how much of Marion's charm and sweetness with all these parents and the staff was genuine, and how much was just a pose. He had come ruefully to the conclusion that however close you were to a person you never discovered what was in their innermost heart. But Marion had helped his success with Arrowhurst, and brought him much happiness; he was grateful, and if he ever remembered that a perfect union was what he hoped for from marriage, he also never forgot what he owed to her loyalty, hard work and skill.

Marion liked meeting people. Her father had been a diplomat, and when she was a girl she had developed an ease of manner with everyone she met which proved invaluable to her now. She devoted a lot of time and thought to her task, and she had the assurance and satisfaction that came from knowing she did it supremely well. She was tall, auburn-haired, and elegant. Timid parents were a little nervous of her until they felt her charm; the bolder ones were gently dragooned and controlled, and told each other how lucky they were in their headmaster's wife— such a delightful woman. No one dared query a request for new socks or more sheets if Marion was its author.

When she left them to talk to someone else, Dick Butler and Ronald Cross, the two new masters, gravitated together in a corner by the bookcase. Dick was short and sturdy; his head was round and his hair was red; his nose was sharp and pointed, and he thought well of himself. Ronald was by contrast tall and angular, with floppy fair hair that was much too

16

long. He was fond of chamber music, and was just now engaged upon writing a very obscure, intense novel that was doomed, had he but known it, to remain obscure and unpublished.

The two young men exchanged information about where they lived and what schools had been privileged to educate them; then conversation flagged, until Ronald expressed doubt about his ability to control a class of ten small boys tomorrow.

"Easy," said Dick, with sublime confidence. "Make sure they know who's boss. They soon understand. You've got to treat them like animals."

"More likely they'll make me know they're the boss," said Ronald gloomily, and then, his face brightening, "I say, who's that?"

Dick followed his glance across the room to where Marion was talking to a slight, delicate-looking girl with dark hair.

"Oh, she's Jennifer Wayne, the music mistress," said Dick, pleased to be in a position to impart information. "Of course, you weren't at dinner, or you'd have met her."

"No." Ronald's failure to catch the right train had already earned him a mild rebuke from Geoffrey.

"She's new this term, too," added Dick.

"All right, as well," approved Ronald admiringly.

Dick had already discovered that Jennifer was three inches taller than himself, so now he did not follow as the other young man made his way immediately towards her. Without reserve, Ronald introduced himself and began to talk about a concert he had attended the previous week. Jennifer listened with interest, and smiled once at something he said; seeing her across the room Peter Farquhar thought, in a startled way, that she was lovely. The telephone rang, and as Marion left the room to answer it Jennifer, glancing up, encountered his frank stare; without haste she looked away and gave her attention to what Ronald was saying.

Marion returned in a few minutes.

"Peace again for a while," she said. "Peter, be a dear and get me some more coffee. That's my cup on the mantelpiece."

"Yes, of course," said Peter. He took

Marion's cup and filled it from the large Cona.

"Was that Mrs. Wilson on the telephone?" he asked as he handed it to her.

"No, she never telephones," said Marion. "Peter, you've been introduced to Jennifer, haven't you? See if she'd like some more coffee." Marion believed in discarding formality at once with new members of the staff, especially the young. Christian names helped in the swift development of easy friendliness.

"Yes, of course," said Peter now, once more, delighted to obey.

"Oh, thank you. Yes, please," said Jennifer. Her voice was surprisingly low, rather husky.

"I suppose lots of parents ring up?" she asked Marion.

"Mostly just the mothers of new boys," she was told. "And they're very apologetic as a rule. But I'm sure they are anxious— after all, Tommy and Johnny are their— well, I was going to say ewe lambs, but that isn't quite right—and probably haven't been away from home before, so they may well be worried. But that was Mrs. Jones. She has four sons, and I think we shall have her telephoning us on the first night of term for ever!"

"Both the Jones boys are in fine form," said Peter. "But young Wilson looked a bit doleful. Poor chap, he just sat staring out of the train window all the way down. His mother would be quite justified in telephoning."

"She never has," said Marion.

"He's an only child, isn't he?" said Peter. "I expect he gets rather a fuss made of him at home."

"I wonder," said Marion. She turned to Jennifer. "Mrs. Wilson is one of our more famous parents. She's Janine Dufay, the actress."

"Oh, really? Of course I've heard of her, but I don't think I've ever seen her," said Jennifer.

"She's quite good, I think, though I've only seen her once on the stage," Marion said. "She's a pretty creature. She hasn't been down here at all."

"She was at Victoria," said Peter. "The boy isn't very like her, he's so dark and pale. We don't know what his father's like, do we?"

"No," said Marion. "We just assume

he's a bad lad, as he skipped off to America years ago, leaving Janine stranded. But I think she's well looked after financially, and in any case she must make a lot of money herself."

"What a terrible thing," said Jennifer. "How sad."

"Oh well, it's always happening," said Marion. "I think Mrs. Wilson might well be a handful. Parents are a nuisance. It's quite a job to remember which are the original couples and who are still together."

"I forget about them," said Peter with a smile. "The boys are our concern, not their parents."

"But doesn't it help to understand the boy if you know something about his background?" asked Jennifer with some spirit. "You were saying just now that this boy, Wilson, is homesick. I'm not surprised, if he and his mother are alone together at home. I wonder why she doesn't telephone?"

"Iron self-control," said Peter.

"I doubt it," said Marion. "I have a hunch that she has other fish to fry."

21

"How is Wilson tonight?" Peter asked Marion. "Has he settled down?"

"I think so," she replied. "Phyllis didn't mention him. She told me Matron said that there was just one new boy who was a little weepy, Johnson, and that was because his mother hadn't packed a toothbrush for him. He cheered up when one was found."

The telephone bell rang again then, and with a rueful smile she left them.

"Poor little boys, it must seem very strange at first," said Jennifer. "They're so young."

"Does it seem strange to you?" asked Peter.

She looked at him then, searchingly, as he remembered she had done earlier when they first met before dinner. She had large grey eyes, he saw.

"A bit," she confessed. "I can't help being a little scared. It's my first post."

"You'll be all right," said Peter, and, looking at her, he knew that she would. There was an air of quiet strength about her, unlike the mannered control of Marion, and different also from the pretty poise of Mrs. Wilson. He frowned.

Somehow he could not get the thought of the boy Christopher out of his head.

Jennifer was looking at him curiously, so he smiled and began to ask her how she had spent the holidays. But that night before he went to bed Peter looked in upon Dormitory Four where Christopher slept. He walked past the narrow beds with their silent, sleeping forms. Outside, the rain had stopped, and now the moon cast a pale radiance into the room. It showed the figures of the boys, some sleeping curled up, almost invisible; one lying on his back, arms outflung, with the rounded face of an angel; another lay face downwards, so that one would expect that he must suffocate.

Christopher's bed was in the furthermost corner of the room. There was something about the boy's stillness that told Peter that he was not asleep. He waited for a minute, wondering whether to speak, until the pretence became too much for Christopher. He rolled over and stared up at the young man, and when he saw who it was a look of relief crossed his face, and a sigh like a sob escaped him.

"I—I wasn't blubbing, sir," Christopher began at once.

Peter looked at the small blotched face whose owner had run dry of tears.

"No, of course you weren't, Wilson," he said. He sat down on the end of the bed. "You know, I used to get homesick," he said conversationally, in a whisper. "It isn't anything to be ashamed of, it's just something to try and manage. It'll get easier, you'll see."

"You see, sir, my mother's all alone, and she's bound to miss me badly," Christopher explained earnestly.

"Yes, of course she will, but she wants you to be happy here, and work hard. That's what you must do," said Peter.

"Yes, sir. I know, sir," said Christopher sadly. "I will."

Peter found a useful toffee in his pocket.

"Here, have a sweet," he said. "But don't tell Matron." He got up and smoothed the rumpled bedclothes. "Goodnight, old chap."

Christopher allowed himself to be tucked up. He was desperately tired. Automatically he began to chew the toffee. By the time Peter had reached the door he was asleep.

2

GRAN had sent Christopher a large tin of sweets just before he returned to school; he had put them in the bottom of his trunk himself, between his cricket shoes and his white games sweater, so that was all right. There would be enough to ensure his weekly ration of grub, anyway for most of the term, and perhaps later she would come to see him and bring further supplies. Christopher had lived with Gran for most of his short life, because mother had been too busy acting to have him with her for long, and father was an unknown quantity somewhere in America, an unkind man who had abandoned mother and Christopher a long time ago. He must have been horrid to do such a thing, although he always sent Christopher lovely presents for his birthday and Christmas, and though Gran, who was his mother, was so nice. Lately Gran had been ill, and had been forced to sell her country house in

Buckinghamshire where Christopher had spent so much time. She had gone to live in Cumberland with her daughter, Aunt Freda, whose husband was a parson and who lived in a large house with her three sons and two daughters. Gran had explained to Christopher at Christmas, which was the last time he had seen her, that she was an old lady and not well enough to live alone; and that now he was such a big boy and away at school they would in any case see less of one another. She had promised that he would often stay with her at Aunt Freda's, but last holidays the cousins had all had measles and so he had not gone.

Letters were the next anxiety. The post was handed out every day in the dining-room after breakfast. Each morning Christopher was certain that today there would be a letter from mother, or anyway a card, but one never came. Gran sent him a postcard every week, and sometimes a letter, but it wasn't the same. Peter, whose task it often was to give out the letters, slowly as the term got under way realised that he seldom had anything to hand Christopher; and as soon as he began to watch for it he noticed the pinched look on the little boy's face, and the droop of the small shoulders when it was clear that there was again nothing for him.

The golden rule for schoolmasters and schoolmistresses is not to discriminate; but there are always some children who attract or who need more attention than others. Peter became haunted by the lonely figure of Christopher trudging across the playing field, bat in hand, to cricket. He did not teach the smallest boys, so they never met in class, but out of school hours their paths occasionally crossed. The other boys were not unkind to Christopher; they did not bait or bully him; they simply took no notice of him, for he had little to say and nothing to contribute. They were quite willing to include him in their activities, but they did not exert themselves to draw him in, and the anxious Christopher was always on the fringe of whatever was going on. But whenever he met Peter the small boy's face lit up with a timid smile; he did not forget the young man's tact, and the toffee, on the first night of term.

Peter himself was busy. The term's routine developed; he had many responsibilities, and he was occupied for at least twelve hours every day. There was always something to be done; out of school hours there was cricket, and soon swimming would begin; he was also increasingly helping Geoffrey with the administrative side of the school. His work had always been to Peter wholly absorbing, but this term there was a new element: Jennifer. Peter found that he spent a lot of time thinking about her, and hoping to meet her in the passage.

One Saturday afternoon, when the term was a few weeks old, a cricket match was in progress. Peter umpired the first half, but after tea he was free. It was a sunny day, but the May breeze was fresh. Round the cricket pitch tall trees cast swaying shadows on the grass. Arrowhurst, all out for 107, were determined to defeat their opponents by brilliant fielding and bowling, and took the field briskly.

Jennifer had been sitting with Judy Palliser, one of the assistant matrons, lazily watching the match from a patch of shade under the trees. When her companion left because she must go and find clean shirts for the boys for Sunday, Peter came to take her place beside Jennifer. He winced as Jones I, the best bowler that Arrowhurst could boast and brother of the car-sick one, sent down his first ball wide.

"Will we get them all out?" asked Jennifer.

"Not if that's the best that Jones can do," said Peter with a grin. He stretched his long legs out on the grass, and for a time they sat in companionable silence watching the play. Round them the school looked at the match in a restive manner, the keen spectators scoring, and the others writhing and tumbling about in the nearest approach to sitting still that small boys ever achieve.

"How are you getting on?" Peter asked suddenly. "Are you liking it here?"

"Yes, very much," said Jennifer. "I'm getting used to it now. The boys are pretty good on the whole. I was very fierce to begin with; now I find I can let up a bit." She turned to smile at him, and he was struck again by her serenity. It was hard to imagine her being in the least ferocious.

"Don't you ever get tired of 'The Merry Peasant'?" he asked.

Jennifer laughed. "I keep hoping to discover a budding Pouishnoff," she said.

"I doubt if you'll find one here," he replied.

"Well, there are one or two hopefuls, but no prodigies so far," she answered. "It's a bit discouraging for them till they've learnt enough to start getting some pleasure from playing."

"How about singing? I heard some stalwart grenadiers yesterday," said Peter.

"Oh, did you?" She was amused. "I like to encourage those sort of songs, as well as gentler or more classical things. We're doing some Gilbert and Sullivan too. We have got one boy with a beautiful voice, you know, something really special."

"Oh, who?" Peter asked with interest.

"It's Wilson. He seems such a quiet, sad little boy; isn't he the one you thought was so homesick?" Jennifer turned her large grey eyes upon Peter, and for a moment he forgot what they were talking about because he found her so entrancing.

"Oh—really—has he?" Peter picked a blade of grass and pulled himself together.

"Yes, I think so. He always tries so hard, poor little chap. No one plays the triangle with more determination or beats the drum so vigorously in the band; but when he sings he doesn't need to try, it just comes, in the purest tone. He doesn't know it, of course. It's about the only thing he seems good at. I'd like to put him in the choir."

Peter looked doubtful. "He's a bit young. We usually wait till they're in the third form," he said.

"I know. I wanted to ask you if we could make an exception for Wilson," said Jennifer.

"If he's as good as all that perhaps we should think about it," said Peter. "It might help him all round to have some encouragement like that. I'll talk to Geoffrey about it. We'd probably have to put another second former in too."

"Jones is good," said Jennifer.

"All the Joneses are very musical," said Peter. "Really Welsh, they are. I don't see why Wilson and Jones II shouldn't go into the choir, they can both read all right. I'll let you know what Geoffrey says."

"Thank you," Jennifer said.

"I wonder if Wilson's settling down at all," said Peter. "He always seems to be on his own. This is his third term, and one would have expected him to be used to things by now."

"I don't think he is homesick," said Jennifer. "There's something else wrong. I wondered if it was his background—you said his parents were separated. It must affect him somehow, surely?"

"He doesn't seem to get many letters," Peter said, "just postcards from his grandmother."

"I gather he works harder than any boy in his form, yet he never comes higher than seventh or eighth," said Jennifer. "How little one knows what's going on in their heads."

"In some ways it's a shattering responsibility to have charge of them in their formative years like this," said Peter. "You tend to think of them simply as little animals, to be fed, controlled and exercised, and have their heads crammed with selective knowledge, Common Entrance fodder. But every one of them is very much an individual."

"And quite a few of them are probably going through their own little bit of hell," said Jennifer.

"Thank goodness most of them seem to live simply for the moment," said Peter with a smile. "Weren't you happy at school, Jennifer?"

"I hated it," she said. "I couldn't bear the lack of privacy. There was never any time to yourself, and nowhere to be alone."

"What made you take up teaching, then?" he asked. "It's not very easy, ever, in a school, to get away from other people."

She laughed. "Well, it can be done, if one's determined," she said, "and it's different from this angle. In any case, it was the only way I could have a musical career. But I like it, I'm intrigued by all the children. Now that I know their names it's much more interesting."

"Do you really know them all?" asked Peter.

"Oh, yes, I've known them for ages," she said with some pride. "There was a group of nondescript ones I found very muddling, but it didn't take me long to learn the naughty ones, and the blonds and the three redheads. Of course, some of them thought it a great joke to pretend to be each other, but I've got them taped now."

He looked at her with admiration. There was a dusting of minute freckles across the bridge of her straight nose. She, in her turn, noticed a tiny scar, almost invisible, on his lean cheek.

"I'm so glad Miss Macnab left last term," said Peter.

Jennifer smiled. "Was she the one who walked like a headmaster?" she asked.

"What can you mean?" He burst out laughing.

"I think it was Sparrow who said she did," Jennifer told him demurely. "I gather she wasn't popular."

"She was rather too strict, but a good soul," said Peter. "Now that I come to think of it she did often walk with her hands behind her back, like Geoffrey, and took powerful strides. She was rather the hearty, hockey type."

"Poor Miss Macnab," said Jennifer.

Christopher had been watching the match from a point of vantage fifty yards away. Perhaps if he ever got into the First Eleven his mother would come and watch him play; but it seemed very unlikely that he would ever manage it. So far he had never made more than six runs, and any catch that came his way he dropped, while as for bowling—he could not bear to remember the ignominy of his last effort. Thank goodness Mr. Farquhar had taken him off after two ghastly overs. Mr. Farquhar was jolly decent, he never made fun of a fellow for being a mutt, that was one thing. If everyone was like him it wouldn't be so hard to do things; he seemed to expect that you'd be able to, and even though you couldn't quite, somehow your bishes didn't matter. Instead of laughing at him yesterday for being run out, as Mr. Butler would have done, Mr. Farquhar had said: "Well done, Wilson, that was a sporting try," and Christopher's face had been saved. There was Mr. Farquhar now, sitting under the beech tree with Miss Wayne. In an undefined way Peter was a friend, and Jennifer another. Christopher did not understand why he enjoyed her classes. He was too young to realise his own musical gift; vaguely, if he thought about it, he felt she was nice and never mocked anybody, even redheaded Roberts who sang every song on one dreary note, approximately Middle C, with no deviation whatsoever.

He thought about swimming. If the weather stayed chilly it would be some weeks before they were allowed into the sea. Sparrow said it was usually the middle of June, unless the summer was exceptionally warm. It was silly to worry about it yet. Christopher, until he went to Arrowhurst, had only ever in his life spent one week at the sea. It had been last year, with mother. She had not bathed; she had basked in the sun in her white swimsuit while Christopher dabbled in the shallows. Mother had not minded because he did not want to swim, she had simply not noticed; and no one knew how appalled he had been by the vastness of the ocean. Even to watch other children disporting themselves had unnerved him. The thought of entrusting his whole person to the waves was more than he could endure. His summers, before this, had always been spent at Gran's and, though she had sometimes said he must learn to swim, nothing had ever happened about it because she lived so far inland. He wondered how long it took to learn. Mother would be very pleased if he could do it quickly. It would be lovely to report success in his Sunday letter. He was always hoping to write that he had come first or second in form, but although he tried his hardest he had still never risen higher than seventh.

When his thoughts arrived at this depressing point there was a loud crack as the batsman hit a ball from Jones I a resounding thwack. It sailed into the air and dropped to the ground just short of the boundary in front of him. The moment crystallised for Christopher. He stared at the ball as it raced over the line across the grass towards him. He glanced frantically to right and left, but there was no other boy within three feet of him. He knew he must stop the ball and return it to the game. He crouched, and cupped his hands in its path. Still travelling very fast, it brushed against his wrist, stinging it, tore through the space between his heels and continued on into the long grass behind him. He hurried to fetch it, tears of mortification in his eyes, but Roberts had already moved from further down the field, and with easy nonchalance he threw the ball to the nearest fielding Arrowhurst boy. He did not trouble to speak to Christopher, who was thankful to be spared audible derision, but the pitying look on his freckled face was bad enough. Christopher sat down again and stared hard at the ground, invisible at first through the mist of his tears, but as he blinked steadily his eyes cleared. He saw two ants, busily scurrying along, winding their way in and out of the grasses; they bustled off on unknown urgent errands. Christopher thought about them very hard, so that he could ignore the agony of humiliation that made him feel as though his tummy was on fire. Presently he got up, and, stuffing his hands in his pockets, walked round the field to a place where, behind a crowd of bigger boys, he would be safe from another such exposure. He looked across the green aertex backs in front of him at the white figures on the field, and emptied his mind of everything else. He had learned now that by fierce concentration upon some other subject he could almost forget that the terrible moment had ever happened. It would lie in wait for him, lurking in a corner of his memory, ready to pounce out if he relaxed his guard for an instant, or if any new mortification befell him. Christopher forced his imagination outwards. He identified himself with the boy who was batting; so time passed until the match was over.

Geoffrey sat rather splendidly in a deckchair outside the pavilion. A young master from the visiting school was beside him, timidly talking. Geoffrey, in middle age, was a distinguished-looking man. He was tall and well-proportioned, and now that his thick hair was greying his appearance was nearly as good as that of Marion. She, too, was sitting watching the match. The visiting master found her a distinct contrast from his own headmaster's wife, who was a harassed, hard-working, tweedy sort of person, very kind indeed and adored alike by boys and staff. Marion he found remote, and he felt nervous of her elegance. She wore a narrow, tan worsted skirt, a cream silk shirt which was just the right shade to set off her auburn hair, and a flecked tweed jacket. Her long, slim, nylon legs ended in expensive handmade shoes.

Geoffrey was on the whole complacent. The opposing wickets were falling fast, and there would anyway be a moral victory as the score was 41 for 8 already, even if time did not allow the last two men to be despatched. Jones I had settled down after two bad overs, and the fielding had been consistently good; altogether it was a successful afternoon. They had now got through the first three weeks of term without an infectious illness appearing; unless some wretched parent exposed its son to evil germs on a day out all should be well for the term. The two new young masters had settled down; Ronald Cross, although he looked unpromising, was making a success of the young brigands in the second form; Butler seemed enthusiastic and effective as a disciplinarian, though Geoffrey could not yet find him likeable as an individual. Jennifer Wayne appeared content; it was a long time since the organ in chapel had been played by anyone with such musical ability and talent.

They could look forward to a good summer.

Phyllis Norton, who alone did more to

make Arrowhurst School run smoothly than any other person, sat on a bench among the boys and allowed herself a cursory glance at Geoffrey. Officially the secretary, she was in fact the most powerful member of the staff. She kept the peace amid the matrons; she paid the bills and totted up the fees; she sent out the reports and found new cooks; under the presidency of Marion she oversaw the housekeeping. She had been in love with Geoffrey for fifteen years, ever since he had returned to Arrowhurst, then evacuated to Wales, during the war. He had been badly wounded in the lung and invalided from the Army. Now no one would have known how ill he had been at that time, but he was still far from robust, and could take no active part in the sporting side of school life; all that devolved upon Peter.

Those first years had, for Phyllis, been the best. Then she had hoped for a future with Geoffrey. He had become headmaster with unexpected suddenness when old Mr. Frost, his uncle, had died of a stroke. In those days he had relied upon Phyllis to provide answers to the problems which in his inexperience he could not solve himself. Then, one September term, he had brought Marion to Arrowhurst. Phyllis, anguished, had wanted to leave, but she could not, for still he needed her; and by the time he could have spared her she was used to her hurt, and no longer had the will to take herself away. So she remained, and in a way was content. Marion too relied on her, often deferring to her rather charmingly over domestic matters; and Phyllis despised herself because she could not, even after all this time when Geoffrey was clearly happy and devoted to his wife, really like her.

Under her tree, Phyllis moved on the hard bench and sighed. She would still be here, ordering the food and typing out exam. papers, until she grew too old to be of any use. She knew that she could never have done for Geoffrey what Marion had achieved. No amount of devotion could have made up for the success she had brought and for the confidence she had given him. She had added the polish to Arrowhurst, lifting it from being just another very good prep. school into being, some said, the best. Phyllis was deeply thankful for Geoffrey's happiness, even though she regretted not being the instrument of it. She did not realise how much of Marion's calm was owed to the fact that Phyllis had for years spared her the small, domestic tribulations of most headmasters' wives.

Sometimes Phyllis wondered if Geoffrey minded having no children of his own. On the whole she thought not; there were enough boys here to fill that gap, and Marion was not a maternal person. Her approach to the boys, while always kind, was never touched with sentiment; the marriage might well have been less successful if there had been the natural result of a family.

Phyllis knew that her own life held many compensations; she had many friends; she loved the boys; and she was useful. Though sometimes lonely, she need never be alone among so many people.

Dick Butler was a witness of Christopher's failure to retrieve the cricket ball.

Silly young wet, thought he. In Dick's opinion Wilson was a complete and utter drip, nine years old and unable to catch the simplest ball, run fifty yards without stumbling, or perform the most straight-forward mathematical calculation. Always mooning about the place, a dead loss in every way, Wilson needed a sharp shock to pull him together. He was a spoiled Mummy's boy, if ever there was one.

Marion sat with her mind a complete blank. Cricket bored her, but she enjoyed the smug satisfaction that came from watching it because she ought. If she bothered to think at all, it was only to register mild annoyance that her stocking had caught on a splinter of her chair and drawn a thread. She would ask Phyllis to enquire in Charnton about those new garden chairs of tubular steel. Poor old Phyl; there she was, across the field, sitting among the boys. Marion saw her glance across at Geoffrey; she was still eating her heart out for him, and he quite unaware. Marion felt a comfortable twinge of pity for Phyllis, and a corresponding increase in her own complacence.

She saw Jennifer and Peter get up from their place on the grass and walk slowly round the field. Presently they turned and began to walk back, faces earnestly towards each other as they talked. That was entirely suitable, if anything should come of it. Peter would, in due course, succeed Geoffrey as headmaster, and Jennifer could easily be groomed as her own successor. Marion had often feared that Peter might be the victim of an unsuitable attraction; as she told Geoffrey, who laughed at her fears about the assistant matrons, propinquity is a great match-maker, and most of these girls were only filling in a term or two before moving on to something more exciting. Few had a sense of vocation where the children were concerned.

As she arrived at this point in her mental peregrinations Jones I, bowling again, took a deep breath. He pounded up to the wicket and delivered the ball unerringly on to the middle stump. All out for 57, and Arrowhurst had won the first big match of the summer.

Ronald Cross had spent that sunny afternoon alone in the library, gloomily writing his gloomier novel.

3

"WATER FUNK, water funk, Wilson is a water funk!" chanted Roberts and Jones II, capering in their swimming trunks on the sands before Christopher.

He shivered. Advancing, he stood with the icy sea lapping his ankles, thin arms tight by his sides, unable to step further into the water. Roberts and Jones ran in and out of the sea beside him; forbidden by the school rules to splash him, they made as much commotion as they dared with their limbs, so that showers of cold droplets fell upon Christopher's bony little body. The sea heaved and fell back with the motion of a gentle swell; it was not rough, but to him the small waves seemed tempestuous. He managed a few more steps till he stood knee-deep; then he stuck.

Dick Butler was in charge of this bathing party, the third of the term. On both the others Christopher's antipathy to the ocean had not passed unnoticed; Dick's sympathies were with Roberts and Jones.

"Come along, Wilson, in with you," he said now, striding purposefully towards Christopher.

"Oh sir, oh, please sir!" Christopher's teeth chattered and he looked blue.

"Of course you're cold, standing there shivering," exclaimed Dick. "Get wet, can't you? You'll soon warm up."

Christopher stood as though paralysed.

"Here, give me your hand," said Dick. He took hold of Christopher's reluctant wrist and pulled him out into the water, so that it caught him round the waist with freezing hands. On his other side, Roberts enthusiastically seized his arm. Between them, they caused the petrified little boy to stumble. He fell, and the water rushed over his head and up his nose and into his eyes. Dick pulled him to his feet, dropped his hand, and said briskly, "There, now you're in. Splash about, Wilson," and went off to break up a ducking party that had begun a few yards away, swimming up to the protagonists with confident, powerful strokes.

Christopher thought he was drowning. The water was level with his chest, and as each wave came it caught him off balance; he spluttered, swaying, struggling to keep his feet, unable to see for the water in his eyes, his arms bent up like little wings under his ears. Then, with gasping breath, he began to scream.

Peter, who had arrived upon the beach in time to witness the whole scene, was beside him in a few seconds. Until he had pulled Christopher back to shallow water he was not aware of the boy's identity.

"Stop that noise," said Peter sternly. Christopher choked, and managed to control his screams; he began to sob instead. Peter looked from him to the other boys who were watching, some with round, shocked eyes, and some with giggles ill-suppressed. The only way to help Christopher now was to send him out of the sea at once.

"Go and get your clothes on," he said shortly.

Thankfully, Christopher raced out of the water and up the beach. Peter stood in the sea, a lean, muscular figure in his bathing trunks, with his hands on his hips, surveying the other boys. They looked a trifle guilty, and fell to swimming and splashing with great vigour. Peter turned over in his mind whether to deliver a dressing-down; at length he decided that the chilly sea was not the place for one, and that Dick Butler was in any case the worst offender.

Jennifer came down the cliff path to see Christopher run weeping up the beach. She had not been down before to watch the boys swim; they went in batches according to form and ability, carefully timed and watched, about ten at a time. She saw Peter in the water, very tall beside these smallest boys, the "non-swimmers," setting two to swim the distance between two rocks which formed a preliminary test of competence, and which, when passed, allowed them to graduate into a higher group. She sat on a boulder to watch, and then remembered Christopher. He was struggling stickily into his clothes, twenty yards away, little pink back modestly turned. She longed to help him, but was sure it would be a mortal blow to his pride if she did. At last, when he was almost clothed, she went over to him. His teeth were still chattering. He looked at her as though he did not recognise her, and he was crying as well as shivering. Jennifer thought it was best to ask no questions.

"Put your jersey on, Wilson, and we'll look for crabs," she said calmly.

Without replying, Christopher did as he was told. Jennifer thought he should be made to run briskly up and down the beach to warm up, but he looked incapable of running anywhere. She wondered what had gone wrong, and felt a little wave of anger that Peter should allow the child to be alone on the beach in this distress, for it was quite by chance that she had come along. They walked to a pool among the rocks, and Jennifer fished about finding shells, and a small white crab who scuttled about in the depths.

The other boys were coming up the beach now, shouting and laughing, their bathe finished. Peter and Dick Butler ran with them over the sand to where they had left their clothes. Then, with a towel flung round his shoulders, Peter came towards Jennifer and Christopher. When he had almost reached them he called, "Jenny, could you come here a minute?"

She went at once, ridiculously touched by his diminution of her name, but still a little angry.

"Will you take Wilson back to school? Keep him with you till the others come up. I want to speak to them," he said.

"All right, Peter." She looked at him, puzzled; his face was rather stern, but he smiled abstractedly at her, and then turned away.

"Come along, Wilson, let's take these shells up to school, and then you can help me get some music ready for tomorrow," she said.

Silently, Christopher began to follow her up the beach and towards the path which twisted up the cliff.

"I like this one best," said Jennifer, selecting one of the shells to show him, in an effort to divert him. Christopher could not reply. He sniffed loudly.

"For goodness' sake blow your nose, Christopher," she exclaimed then, in exasperation.

Whether it was the touch of impatience in her tone that unmanned him again, or the sudden use of his Christian name, Christopher could not have said, but suddenly the thoughts he had held away firmly flooded upon him once more, and his tears flowed. This was too much for Jennifer, and she was ashamed of her moment of irritation. They were half-way up the path now, and screened by an overhang of rock from the people on the shore. He was only a little boy of nine, and she put her shells on the ground, sat down and caught him on to her lap. Christopher sobbed and sobbed, clutching at her with frantic, desperate hands. Jennifer began to fear that they would still be there when Peter and the others climbed the path, and she was quite sure this was not the sort of behaviour schoolmistresses should encourage in their charges. She found a handkerchief and said, "Here, have a good blow," pressing it into his hand.

Christopher managed to obey, and some control came back to him. Jennifer helped him to his feet and took his hand. They continued up the path, hand in hand, and when they reached the top she let him go. He blew his nose again and achieved a watery smile.

Deciding that least said was soonest mended, she gave him a little push.

"Race you to the house," she said. Side by side they ran, then, over the tussocky grass of the headland and in to school by the open side door. Christopher, panting, had some colour by the time they stopped, and turned to laugh at Jennifer as she caught up with him.

"I beat you, Miss Wayne," he said.

"Yes," said Jennifer. "Well done. Now, come on, we'll sort out those songs."

She led the way to the music room where her piano lessons took place, and Christopher became animated as they discussed what would be needed for class tomorrow. Jennifer played him a few bars of a new song she had found, and with complete lack of self-consciousness he began to sing the verse, reading the words with some hesitancy, but grasping the melody at once.

"Well sung," said Jennifer, as they finished. "We'll do it again."

Christopher's eyes were sparkling. She played the introductory passage, and, eagerly, he began to sing a bar too soon.

"Wait for it," she said with a smile. Then she lifted her hands from the keys.

"You aren't reading the music, are you?" she asked.

He shook his head.

"Well, you see, there are four beats in the bar, like we have in band," she explained. "Look, you count them and follow the notes as I play. These black ones are full beats, and these with little feet are halves." She counted it out to him. He understood at once, and made no mistake when she played it again. He sang the little song through with her, his voice soaring, a pure, sweet sound in the small room. Watching the music carefully, he turned the page for her, and sang on, flushed and happy, to the end.

They smiled at one another then.

"Well!" said jennifer. "I wish the others could sing like you. You ought to learn the piano. Would you like to?"

"I—I don't know. I hadn't thought. Yes, I would," he decided in a burst.

"Why don't you ask your mother if you can start next term?" she suggested, rising and closing the book.

A tight, closed look came over Christopher's face.

"I might," he said dully.

Jennifer saw that the light had gone out of him. She looked puzzled, and was about to speak when the door opened and in came Peter.

"Ah, Wilson," he said, with a smile at Christopher so that the boy would know he was not in disgrace. Jennifer realised that he meant her to go and leave them together. She picked up a pile of music.

"That was a great help, Wilson, thank you," she said, and went out.

Peter did not know what he should say to Christopher. It was no good, though, abandoning the situation as it was. He had said very little to the boys on the beach; he did not want to add to Christopher's troubles by making him the cause of punishment. He blamed Dick Butler for what had happened, and had commanded that young man to attend him in the study after dinner.

Christopher stood first on one leg and then the other. The magic of his few minutes' singing with Jennifer had disappeared. He looked, as so often, lost and forlorn, but he was never afraid of Peter.

"I'm sorry, sir," he said humbly.

Peter, who was seldom at a loss for words, found something to say.

"You don't want to go on being scared of the sea, do you?" he asked.

"No, sir." Christopher hung his head, staring at his dusty sandals.

"Don't you ever go to the sea for holidays?"

"No, sir. Well, I did once, but I didn't bathe, only paddled. Mummy—Mummy didn't bathe either."

"I see. Well, most of the others have seaside holidays every year, they're used to it. It does take a bit of getting used to," Peter said, and paused.

"It's so big," Christopher suggested.

"Yes, but you're only being asked to go into one small bit of it," Peter pointed out. "You have got to get used to it, Wilson. You know that, don't you?"

Christopher nodded.

Peter turned his back and walked over to the window.

"Being brave means not showing it when you're afraid of something," he said casually, gazing out. "It isn't being brave to go into the sea if you like bathing; but if it frightens you, and you pretend it

doesn't, that's being brave. D'you understand?" He swung round then to look at
Christopher.

"Yes, I think so, sir," he said.

"If you go a little further in each time,
you'll soon stop minding, and when you
can swim you'll enjoy it," Peter said.

"I want to swim," said Christopher
earnestly. "Mother would be pleased."

"Of course she would. You'll soon learn
if you really try," Peter declared. "Now,
I'll help you, and so will the other masters,
but you'll have to do most of it yourself.
We can't teach you unless you'll try to
learn. I'll take you in the swimming belt
tomorrow if you'll go into the water
without a fuss. What about it?"

"It was the others, laughing at me, and
splashing," muttered Christopher.

"I've told the others you'll be swimming
with me tomorrow," said Peter, "so if you
don't do it, you'll be letting me down."

Christopher's eyes met his. Peter
thought he had never seen such an old
look on the face of any child.

"All right, sir," he said. "Thank you."

"Good boy. Cut along then, it's time for
tea."

He turned away again as Christopher left the room, and looked out of the window at the sunny garden beyond. He wondered if that had been the right way of dealing with the situation. Poor little kid, he'd had a horrid experience, and he would need a lot of help to overcome this fear. Some people might say he should not be forced into the water, but Peter felt that would only increase the problem; he would become conspicuous, and he would still be afraid. He sighed, and wished Jennifer would come back so that he could discuss it with her. He waited a few minutes, but she did not return, and he had to leave without a chance to talk to her.

Marion had gone to London for the night. She had learned early that the narrow world of school was only tolerable if one escaped from it sometimes, and she punctuated the term with expeditions to her hairdresser, the Academy, the theatre, and other such places of interest. On these occasions Phyllis often had coffee after dinner with Geoffrey in his study. She thought he might be lonely, and she knew he liked to talk shop; she did not flatter herself that her own company brought him any special pleasure. She was able now to be as matter-of-fact with him as if she was another man. She poured out his coffee, and sat opposite him in a large armchair talking about the boys. Part of Phyllis's mind dealt with what she was saying, while a tiny, uncontrolled part flitted wildly about pretending that she sat here every night like this, talking about the school. She often wondered how far Marion entered with him into his dreams; Geoffrey had aspirations for every boy that came to Arrowhurst: the few who lived up to them justified his ambition for the many.

"Then there's Wilson," she said at last.

Geoffrey frowned.

"He's becoming rather a problem," he said.

"Yes." Phyllis considered. "It's his third term, but he seems more unsettled now than he ever did before. He's not eating properly. Matron and I were talking today about getting Alec to look at him."

Alec Hunt was the school doctor, who lived in Charnton.

"I've just had Peter talking to me about

him too," said Geoffrey. "It appears there was a scene on the beach this afternoon. Wilson is afraid of the water."

"Oh, dear!" Phyllis said.

"Yes, it's unfortunate. But it's always the way; the difficult ones never end with one problem." Geoffrey looked at Phyllis. "What shall I do, Phyl? Shall I send for the boy? Peter seems to have treated him like a wise uncle, I think he's on the right lines." He told her what had happened.

"I should leave it to Peter, anyway for a bit, and see how things go," said Phyllis. "You'll make it seem too important if you interfere. We'll leave Alec out of it too, for the moment, the boy's different enough from the main ruck already without our emphasising it. Maybe it's being afraid of the sea that's made him lose his appetite. When he gets over that he'll settle down, I expect."

"Peter's dealing with young Butler, too," said Geoffrey. "Silly young ass, but I suppose he meant it for the best."

"Probably, but it was very stupid, all the same," said Phyllis. "You'd think the parents would accustom their children to the elements before sending them to us.

60

It's asking a lot of a sensitive child like that one to expect him to put on a show in front of a lot of heartless little devils who don't know the meaning of fear."

This was an impassioned speech from Phyllis, and Geoffrey told her so.

She said at once, "I can't help feeling anxious about Wilson, there's something very pathetic about him, and I don't think it's quite like anything we've had to deal with before. He isn't doing this to draw attention to himself, I'm certain; he isn't one of those. I know he's often alone, but the other boys don't dislike him. It's as if he doesn't want to be with them. I'll keep a particular eye on him, anyway."

They went on to talk of other things. It was quiet and peaceful in the study; as it grew darker Phyllis switched on the lamp and drew the dark red curtains across the open windows to keep out the moths and flying beetles. In the distance the unending murmur of the sea made a background to their voices.

Peter was very angry with Dick Butler, who had seldom in his life before received what he thought of as such a rocket.

Sentences about responsibility, bullying, and the future generation flew heatedly about his reddening ears.

"I didn't mean the kid to get a ducking," he protested when at last he could get a word in edgeways. Peter continued to lecture him, however, much angrier in Dick's opinion than the extent of the episode warranted. When at last he was released he felt extremely small, and also very ill-used. No need for Farquhar to get so het up about such a little thing, he thought moodily, slouching off down the passage. Do the little tick Wilson good, there'd be no more nonsense from him now, everyone would see.

So Peter, and in a lesser way Christopher, made a potential enemy of Dick.

Christopher went to sleep early that night. He was so much exhausted physically that his weary mind could not cope with all his worries. There were one or two half-hearted cries of "Here comes the water funk," as he entered the dormitory, but Jones II now came to his defence and said priggishly, "We're not to call him that, Mr. Farquhar said."

"Oh, stale buns," said Robert, piqued at losing his ally. "Anyway he is one, and now I shan't swop my Mauritius stamp I said I would, so there!"

Jones looked crestfallen. Then the role of protector to Christopher, which had occurred to him as a crusade during Peter's brief remarks earlier, appealed to him again.

"I'll give you my black striped hairy caterpillar tomorrow, Wilson, if you like," he offered, and Christopher who loathed caterpillars, knew that he must accept the hand of friendship thus extended.

4

RONALD CROSS sat in the library writing his novel. Whenever he had any time to spare this was his occupation; the pile of manuscript covered in his sprawling handwriting grew slowly larger as the weeks passed. Forgotten were the French exercises of Form II, and their geographic journeys, as he followed his hero through the labyrinths of life in Bohemian Chelsea as he imagined it. He was completely engrossed, and did not hear the door open.

"Ah, Ronald, not got a game this afternoon?" It was Wilfrid Fitzgibbon, the classics master and oldest member of the staff. He was a small, bent man with sparse grey hair and spectacles, and rather hard of hearing. He had, however, an uncanny ear for detecting a boy up to no good.

Ronald came back to earth with a bang.

"No, not this afternoon," he said, pausing with his pen uplifted.

"Hm, pity. You ought to be outside, you know. Doesn't do to work all the time. What's that you're doing, writing a novel?"

"Yes. How did you know?" Ronald asked, with disarming naïvety.

"Everyone writes one sometime or other, or would if they had time," said Wilfrid. "When I was your age I was always writing them. What's it about? London and low life?"

"Yes," said Ronald, taken aback at this perspicacity.

"D'you know a lot about it?" Wilfrid asked.

"Well, quite a bit, and I can imagine—" Ronald said. Wilfrid interrupted.

"Don't let your imagination run away with you," he advised, smiling at Ronald's very innocent appearance. "And don't be too angry, will you?"

Ronald frowned. "Why not?" he asked.

"Life has a lot of good points, you know," Wilfrid said.

"The privileged—" Ronald began vaguely.

"There are few privileges now," said Wilfrid, sitting down. "Except possibly for senior civil servants and members of the Coal Board and the TUC. But I take it those aren't the privileged to whom you refer?"

Ronald shook his head.

"Presumably you went to a school like Arrowhurst, and I seem to recognise your tie," the old man said.

"Yes, but—" Ronald attempted to put in a word, but Wilfrid swept on.

"Most of our parents scrimp and save to send their boys here," he said. "Arrowhurst prefers those boys to the sons of wealthy tycoons. Take the Joneses, for instance, with four sons, two here now, one left last term, and one to come next year. Would you sweep that away?"

"No, but it should be available to everyone," said Ronald.

"It is," said Wilfrid. "There are three boys here now from ordinary council schools, and there are plans to make vacancies available to more. The parents pay almost nothing for them; they have their fees met by bursaries."

The wind was thus smartly removed from Ronald's sails, but he persevered.

"My book isn't about boys," he said, smiling in spite of himself.

"I think it's about a talented young writer, or perhaps painter, who becomes absorbed into a group of young intellectuals, girls in tight trousers with flowing manes, and youth—men I mean—" Wilfrid checked himself before saying "youths"—"with great thoughts about life and freedom of expression."

Ronald began to laugh. "The hero is a playwright," he admitted. "His play shocks London, until everyone realises how right he is about life."

"He was fortunate to get it produced," suggested Wilfrid.

"He met a beautiful young actress, and she helped," said Ronald.

"Ah. Very lucky." Wilfrid nodded.

"How did you guess what it was about?" asked Ronald suspiciously.

"Oh, I was once going to be a real writer, too," said the other. "I started about your age, so I know the sort of lines you'd be working on."

"Why didn't you go on? What happened?" Ronald was shocked.

"Oh, I could never finish the books. No

sooner was one drafted out than I felt inspired to start another, when some fresh aspect of life appealed to me," said Wilfrid. "Then the war came—the 1914 war, that is; and after that I became a schoolmaster and took up gardening."

"And don't you write anything now?" Ronald was very horrified.

"I've given it up," said Wilfrid. "Growing tomatoes and chastising the young is creative enough for me."

He smiled when he saw Ronald's look of dismay.

"But don't let me depress you, my boy," he said. "You may have it in you to write, but if I were you I'd stick to subjects you really know."

"But I know so little," Ronald admitted sadly. "Surely imagination can—"

"Imagination is very useful, allied to facts," said Wilfrid, "and it's a fact that there are still a lot of very pleasant people in the world. It's also a fact, supported by imagination, that the slugs have probably been at my delphiniums again. Come and see."

The young man shrugged: ruefully he gathered up his work; the thread of thought was broken now in any case, and Wilfrid had made him feel uneasy about his theme. He put it aside in his mind and followed the old man out of the building and over the field to the garden that lay below the house.

"Of course, the salt air often scorches the young plants, and the soil here is poor, very poor," said Wilfrid as they walked along. "It's not easy to get good results, but by judicious use of fertiliser and phosphates we manage very well." It was cold outside; a strong wind was blowing off the sea, though this side of the house was sheltered. "It's a challenge, though, a challenge. Ah, just as I thought, tch, tch." Ronald smiled as the old man bent to inspect a delphinium whose leaves were certainly nibbled. "These are some special ones I bought last year," Wilfrid told him. "Of course, I didn't expect them to do anything much this year, but this won't help them. Dear, dear, what a pity. I must lay some more traps for the creatures. Fetch me the Slug Death, Ronald, like a good lad. It's on the shelf in the shed."

He bent to pull out the only weed in view while Ronald obediently set off on his errand. "Writing novels," murmured the old man into a lupin. "Ought to be playing cricket at his age." But he looked up with a pleased smile as Ronald returned from the potting shed with the tin of powder. "That's kind of you, my boy, thanks," he said. "Now, come along. We'll do this first, and then we'll go and look at the tomatoes."

Jennifer, crossing the garden a few minutes later on her way to the lodge where she and the three other women teachers lived, was amused to see Ronald thus incongruously employed. He looked very long and lanky bending low beside tubby Wilfrid and sprinkling slug powder on the ground, while his lock of fair hair flopped forward over his eyes.

"I shall pay any boy who captures twelve slugs, alive or dead, sixpence," Wilfrid declared as they finished.

"Jones II will win," said Jennifer, overhearing. "He's a confirmed bug collector."

"Entomologist, you mean?" said Ronald grandly.

"Don't show off," said Jennifer with a smile.

Ronald laughed. His admiration of

70

Jennifer had grown stronger with the weeks. He still kept trying to impress her, but his own innate niceness rose more often now above his nonsense.

"Where are you off to, Jennifer?" Wilfrid asked.

"I'm going to wash my hair," she told him. "Very dull." She was dining with Peter tonight in Charnton, but she did not tell them that.

"Come and see my tomatoes first," said Wilfrid.

"I'd like to," she said.

Ronald winked at her over the top of the old man's head as they set off beside him towards the greenhouse, where in happy co-operation with the gardener he kept the school supplied with tomatoes throughout the summer. A rich, succulent smell greeted them: the plants were already heavy with the ripening fruit. Wilfrid crooned over them like a mother, seeming to the two young people to know each globe individually. He picked them each one small, ripe tomato, warm and delicious, to eat in that most perfect way fresh from the plant. Presently they slipped away, leaving him still absorbed.

"He's a dear," said Jennifer.

"Yes." Ronald was pensive. "Funny old boy. He used to write, did you know?"

"Yes, I did," said Jennifer. Peter had told her. "Poor Wilfrid. He never made it. But he seems very happy, nevertheless."

"Perhaps I won't make it, either," said Ronald, looking glum.

"How is the book?" asked Jennifer.

"Oh, it's so slow," said Ronald. "I'll never finish it. That's what happened to Wilfrid. He said he never managed to finish one."

"You may," said Jennifer. "If not this one, then the next, perhaps, when you're older."

"I wish you wouldn't chuck my age in my teeth," said Ronald, glaring. "I'm much older than my years, actually. Have dinner with me tonight, Jenny, and I'll prove it."

"I can't," said Jennifer. "I'm already going out. But why don't you ask Judy? She's not on duty, and I'm sure she'd love to come."

"Judy!" Ronald growled. "Now she is young."

"She's as old as you are," Jennifer reminded him.

"Her mother's milk is still wet on her lips," said Ronald dramatically.

Jennifer burst out laughing.

"Oh, Ronald, is that how they talk in your novel?" she said. "Then yours is too. Don't be so silly."

"I'm not silly, I like a woman with some experience," Ronald told her.

"Well, then, I'm no good to you, for I've very little," said Jennifer. "Cheer up."

Ronald walked on, scowling silently, and then suddenly he began to laugh too.

"Oh, Jennifer, I'm sorry," he said. "You're right, I am an ass. My tongue runs off with me. But all the same I wish you would come out with me."

"Well, perhaps I will another time," said Jennifer, relenting. "It's sweet of you to ask me."

"Will you really come one day?" Ronald looked at her so seriously that she regretted her words.

"Yes, and we'll take Judy too," she said brightly.

"No, we won't," said Ronald firmly,

shaking back his hair. "We'll go to a concert. You'd like that."

"Yes, I would," she said. "All right."

Ronald beamed. "I'll get my hair cut in honour of it," he promised, "so you'll be a public benefactress."

Jennifer laughed. Ronald's hair was a general topic and butt in the common-room, where everyone was constantly urging him to have it cut, and even Geoffrey had remarked that when the barber came to do the boys he would have to be included.

Reluctantly he left her when they reached the lodge. Humming to herself, Jennifer walked up the path, between rows of sweetly scented pinks. In spite of the cold wind their fragrance hung on the air, and she sniffed it with pleasure. Ronald was a dear. He knew he was being ridiculous, posing with his long hair and pretending to be sophisticated. Every day he seemed to shed more of his foolishness; soon he would be a delightful person. He was so much more likeable than Dick Butler. There was something about that young man that Jennifer did not like at all, though what it was exactly she did not understand. She knew he did not like Peter. She had heard him holding forth in the common-room to the effect that Peter was too young for so much authority, and too conceited; and she had heard Ronald telling him off for his views in no uncertain terms. From the lofty pinnacle of her twenty-two years, Jennifer decided that being young was very difficult. Then she remembered that soon she would be with Peter, and the growing pains of Ronald and of Dick vanished from her mind.

The weather had changed again, and there was no bathing because the sea was so rough. Christopher, seeing the rollers from his dormitory window every morning, felt a wave of thankfulness that he was to be spared for one more day from his ordeal; but at the same time he longed for the day when, his fears overcome, he would be able to swim, so that his mother would be proud of him, and the terrible words she had said would be wiped from his memory by new sentences of praise.

By day, the now constant company of Jones II made him think less about it, and they spent much time hunting for the insects which Jones so enthusiastically collected. Christopher shuddered over some of the particularly revolting beetles he had to carry about in his handkerchief, but he was grateful to Jones for his championship, and so he meekly obeyed the bossy instructions of his new friend. Jennifer came upon the two boys one break-time, lying on their stomachs in some bushes, while Jones poked about for the maybug chrysalises which he was certain lurked beneath the soil just there.

After she had enquired for the welfare of Jones's famous collection, Jennifer told him that collecting shells could also be rather fun.

"There are lots of different kinds down on the shore. You should look out for them when you're down there next. Do you remember what a lot we found last week, Wilson? I think we left them on the cliff."

"Oh, yes, we did, Miss Wayne," said Christopher, remembering.

"What a pity. Still, never mind, there are plenty more, and you'll soon be swimming again, so you'll be able to get them then," said Jennifer. She had forgiven

Peter in her mind for his apparent callousness to Christopher that day, after he had explained the story to her; but she was still so new to the tough world of little boys that she was not sure if she approved. Now she smiled at the grubby pair before her, with earth on their faces and bracken sticking to their fronts.

"You two are going into the choir," she said to them. "I've just put the new notice on the board. You can see it when you go in," and with another quick smile she left them, walking away over the short grass with her light step, a goddess now to Christopher. Mouth agape, he stared after her, incredulous.

"Oh, bother, that means choir practice every week," grumbled Jones.

Christopher looked at him in astonishment.

"Aren't you glad?" he demanded.

"No, it's boring," said Jones. "Look, here's one, I told you they'd soon be out." Poking with his stick he disinterred a gleaming, mummy-like object.

"Oh, what a fine one," said Christopher dutifully. "Jolly wizard, Jones. Here's the box." He took a matchbox, already prepared and lined with grass, from his pocket, and offered it to Jones, who carefully laid the specimen within.

"Won't your mater be glad?" he persisted.

"What about?"

"About the choir, of course," said Christopher.

"Shan't bother to say," said Jones.

"Would it be swank to say?" asked Christopher, his face falling. Swanking was almost the worst solecism an Arrowhurst boy could commit.

"Oh, not to your mater," said Jones sensibly. "But I shouldn't think she'd take much notice. Mine expects us all to be in it anyway."

He looked gloomy, and took the box containing the maybug from Christopher. "Let's go in. I want to swop this for a grasshopper. Sparrow's got one. We can get another maybug later. Hurry, there's the bell."

Obediently Christopher hastened across the grass beside his friend, as the clang of the first bell sounded. Sure enough, there on the notice board was official confirmation of his appointment to the choir. He was mad with impatience to write to his mother with the stupendous news; he swelled inside with joy. Perhaps he took after mother; she was probably as good at singing as she was at acting. One day he might be a famous singer at Covent Garden Opera, and mother would say proudly, "That's my son . . ."

The second bell went, and while he still day-dreamed his legs carried him at speed into his form-room. Ronald came stalking in with a pile of books under his arm; he went to the tall desk by the blackboard, shaking his long hair back with a typical gesture that the boys had already begun to mimic, though with scant accuracy since theirs was cut so short.

"Page twenty-one," he said loudly, opening his Shorter Latin Primer. "Jones, begin, please."

Christopher heard not one word; he was busy bowing in the glare of the stage lights, and acknowledging the wild applause of the audience. Turning, he went to the wings, and led out upon the stage the beautiful figure of his mother, who kissed him before them all . . .

That night Christopher lay in bed and thought about the shells. They must still be on the cliff path where he and Miss Wayne had left them. What a pity they had been forgotten, Miss Wayne had said. He thought she would like to have them. That afternoon he had written a letter to his mother telling her, in what he hoped were modest terms, that he was a member of the choir. He had used his new italic pen, which he had acquired as a swop for a penknife, and he had done his very best writing. Gratitude to Miss Wayne filled his breast. Mother would be sure to write now and say that she was pleased, and it would all be thanks to Miss Wayne.

Christopher held his breath and listened. All was silent in the dormitory, except for the sound of light breathing. He slid out of bed and stood for a moment, motionless. No one stirred. Quickly he went across the room to the door. It opened with a tiny squeak, and Christopher's heart thumped. A boy moaned in his sleep and rolled over, then he was silent. Christopher gripped the handle and pattered out, then closed the door behind him, very gently.

The landing was in darkness, but on the floor below, where Mr. and Mrs. Frost had their private rooms, a light burned. It must be the middle of the night at least. A door opened downstairs; there was the sound of a woman's voice, and the rustle of taffeta as Marion crossed the hall. Christopher froze; she sounded just like mother dressed for a party. She was up late; perhaps she had just been to one. Was she coming upstairs? He hesitated, holding his breath, ready to slip back into the dormitory, but the door below closed firmly again, and all was quiet.

Christopher dared not go down the forbidden front stairs. He set off, through dark passages where shadows lurked to pounce, towards the steep back stairs that were used by the boys. Once a board creaked under his bare foot; heart pounding wildly, he paused, but everything else was silent. A ribbon of light showed under Miss Norton's door as Christopher crept past, and the faint smell of her cigarette came to him. Phyllis, sitting darning socks, heard nothing. He went on, the noise of his heart sounding so loud in his ears that he thought it must wake everyone. Round the corner by the cupboard where the fire escape apparatus lived he went, and there were the stairs at last. Christopher stretched out a foot and began to descend into the blackness. Step by step, down he went. The building was not completely dark; one or two lights burned in the distance, and the moon was shining in through the long windows. He reached the bottom at last, and his feet met the cold tiles of the lower passage. He crossed to the garden door: it was locked. Biting his lip, Christopher bent and drew the heavy bolt. The door still held. He looked up and realised that there was another bolt far out of his reach. Frightened tears filled his eyes, but he had come so far that he was not going to turn back now. He padded into Form V's classroom nearby, and came out with a chair which he put by the door. As he set it down it banged against his ankle bone, making him wince. He rubbed the place hard, then climbed on to the chair. Standing on tiptoe, he could just reach the bolt. He pulled it down, and in a moment he was outside and running in the moonlight over the damp, dew-covered grass towards the headland.

He found the shells quite easily. His bare feet touched them as he walked cautiously down the narrow pathway. He took a clean handkerchief from his pyjama pocket and tied them into it; then he turned and began to hurry back up the track.

Phyllis folded away her mending and yawned. She rubbed her eyes; they ached; she should have been wearing her spectacles. She moved across to the window of her room and drew the curtain back to look out. It was a fine night, but cold; the moon was nearly full. Something white moved just outside her line of sight; she frowned, then shrugged, supposing it to be a swooping owl. Christopher, intent only on getting back to his dormitory, never noticed the panel of light from her window that fell across the grass behind him.

Peter came into the school building by the gym door. He locked it behind him, and walked slowly up the tiled passage, whistling under his breath. His imagination followed Jennifer into the lodge where he had just left her. He still saw her wide, grey eyes, and the flush on her usually pale cheeks, and his heart sang at the memory of her face. Soon the vision would be gone; at this moment it seemed as if he could never forget the way she had looked at him tonight, but since falling in love he had already discovered, in dismay, that this must happen. How could imagination be so cruel as to deny one the power to conjure up at will the image of the beloved, whilst leaving it a simple matter to visualise almost anybody else, even those with such humdrum faces as the milkman and Jones II. Perhaps, if he remembered hard enough now, he would still be able to picture her in his mind in the morning, before he really saw her sitting at the piano at prayers. Tonight he had nearly kissed her, but at the last moment some instinct had warned him not to hurry her. Her hand, small and cool, had touched his for a moment, and that was all. Peter sighed happily to himself, utterly content. His joyful trance was abruptly shattered when, not looking where he was going, he stumbled into a chair that stood in the passage where no chair ought to be.

Muttering, Peter picked it up and frowned. As he did so, the garden door opened and Christopher stood revealed, paralysed with horror, on the threshold.

Before Peter had recovered from his surprise, Christopher had begun to shiver and to whimper, "Oh, sir, oh, sir," clasping his thin arms to his body round the bundle he held, like a mother with her infant.

"Come in, Wilson." Peter caught hold of Christopher and pulled him inside. He closed the door and bolted it. Then he turned.

"What on earth have you been doing?" he demanded.

Mutely, Christopher held out the bundle. His teeth were chattering, but he was too much shocked and scared to cry.

"They belong to Miss Wayne," he managed to stammer. Peter saw that the now grubby handkerchief was full of shells. This was a moment outside his experience so far, but he realised that Christopher was almost incapable of speech or thought.

"Come along, Wilson. We'll talk about it in the morning," he said, angry now as his wits returned. "Upstairs with you." He propelled Christopher before him along the passage and up the stairs. The boy stumbled once and barked his shin, but he picked himself up and went on without a murmur, numb with panic.

Peter hesitated outside Matron's room, then, as he was about to knock on her door, he remembered that she had gone away for the night to stay with her married niece. He beckoned Christopher to follow, and went on down the passage. When they came to Phyllis's door and he saw that her light was on, relief filled Peter. She would know how to cope with this, and certainly the child needed some sort of rub down. His pyjamas were damp with dew, and he was thoroughly chilled.

"Wait, Wilson," he commanded, and knocked.

"Who is it? Just a moment." Phyllis's voice came muffled from within. In a few seconds she had opened the door, tying her faded pink dressing-gown round her thin waist. A moment's startled astonishment crossed her face as she saw Peter standing there, with the shaking figure of Christopher in very sandy blue and white striped pyjamas beside him, but it was replaced immediately by her usual calm expression.

"Wilson's been out. He's frozen through. Will you see to him and get him back to bed?" Peter's voice was curt.

"Yes, of course," she replied at once. "Come along, Wilson, it's all right, we'll soon have you nice and warm again," she said in a soothing voice. She took his hand and disappeared with him down the passage.

Peter wiped his forehead and leaned against the wall to wait for her. She reappeared briefly for a minute and thrust a hot-water bottle at him.

"Go and fill it, I've put the kettle on in the surgery" she said, and was gone again. Peter went along to the surgery, and just as he was putting the stopper into the full bottle she entered the room.

"He keeps muttering about some shells," she said, taking it from Peter.

"Oh, they're here." Peter showed her the bundle, which he had stuffed in his pocket as he came upstairs. Phyllis took a beaker from the cupboard, and a jar of malted milk, and began to mix a drink with water from the kettle.

"Hand me the aspirins, will you, Peter?" she said as she did this. "Third shelf, left corner."

Peter got them for her, and she disappeared again, carrying the hot-water bottle, the bundle of shells, the drink and an aspirin. Presently she returned, with just the empty beaker.

"He's asleep," she said briefly. "Now for God's sake tell me what he's been up to. Was he sleep-walking? Why the shells?"

"Don't ask me," said Peter. "He says they're Jennifer's. I was coming along the lower passage when he opened the door from the garden and appeared. I don't know which of us was the more surprised."

"Well, now you've a problem," said Phyllis. "What do you make of it?"

"I don't know what to think," said Peter. "I thought you might have an inspiration, Phyl." He looked at her hopefully.

"I have. We need a cup of tea," she said, going to the sink to fill the kettle.

"There's no milk, unless you feel like going down to the larder, or would you like it mixed with Horlicks?" She plugged the kettle in and turned down the switch. "You look as if you need treating for shock, Peter."

"I do," he said. "I've been imagining the most awful things while you've been gone, from pneumonia and funerals to the whole school walking over the cliff in their sleep." He grinned at her, a little sheepishly. "I suppose nocturnal peregrinations are no novelty to you, Phyl?"

"I remember a midnight feast in the orchard about ten years ago, and we've had one or two sleep-walkers prowling round the landings, but this is a new one to me, too," said Phyllis in her matter-of-fact way. She looked completely unruffled.

"I'd better tell Geoff about it in the morning," said Peter, thinking with some relief that he could unload the responsibility on to the headmaster.

"If you do that, he'll have to take some severe disciplinary action," said Phyllis. "I'm not sure that's wise in this case. It wasn't sleep-walking, you know, I'm sure of that, from the way he talked. Before you tell Geoffrey you'd better see the boy and try to find out what he was doing. There's something on that child's mind, and it isn't just shells. He didn't do much explaining just now, only shivered and kept saying they were for Jennifer. I'll have a look at him in the morning, but he'll probably be none the worse after some sleep."

"Any of the others wake up?" asked Peter.

Phyllis shook her head. "Not a sound from them," she said. "I'll have another look at him before I go to bed." She bent to the kettle, which was boiling, and made the tea. "This looks rather beastly," she said, pouring out a cup and offering it to Peter.

"It looks jolly good to me," he said. "Thanks, Phyl."

They sipped in silence for a few minutes, each busy with their thoughts. Then Phyllis said, "It's just as well Matron's away tonight. Somehow I feel that the fewer people who know about this little escapade the better."

"Maybe you're right." Peter looked

doubtful. "He seems to be so homesick," he said slowly.

"Do you think so?" Phyllis asked. "He's unsettled, yes, but I don't think he's homesick."

"Jennifer doesn't either," said Peter.

"His mother never writes to him, does she?" asked Phyllis. "Jennifer was telling me about it. What's she like? I don't remember meeting her. Of course, I've seen her on the stage."

"Oh, I don't know—she seemed quite nice, very made-up, you know—older than one expects," he said vaguely.

"I suppose she's very busy," said Phyllis. "Pity she doesn't find the time to send him a letter or two."

"Yes," said Peter. "Anyway, I'll see him in the morning and try to get out of him what he was up to. Then I'll tell you and see what you think we'd better do."

For a moment Phyllis was carried back to the day thirteen years before when Geoffrey had caught a boy stealing, and had looked at her with the same young, anxious expression on his face that was now upon Peter's.

She said now, as she had then, "You do that. Two heads are better than one."

Peter said hopefully, "You don't think it would be better forgotten and left altogether?" And then, seeing her face, "No, I suppose you're right, it's got to be sorted out." He finished his tea. "Phyllis," he said, "thank God your light was on. I just didn't know what to do."

"Well, I hope you'd have woken me up," she said mildly.

"I can't think what any of us here would do without you," said Peter, made emotional by the varied events of the night.

Phyllis's eyes pricked sharply. She made a business of collecting the cups and rinsing them in the sink.

"Get along with you, Peter. Time you were in bed," she said gruffly.

"Yes." He looked at her, and with the dually sharpened perception of a sensitive nature in love, and reaction from fright, he realised what her life really was, devoted wholly to the service of the school, and the people in it. He saw lines of patience and fatigue, not middle age, upon her face, and a kind of beauty in her homely features.

She turned from putting the cups away, and saw him standing looking at her intently.

"Come along, Peter," she said. "Off you go now. Goodnight."

Dick Butler slept near the top of the back stairs. He heard footsteps pass, and opened his door quietly. Looking out, he saw Peter's back view disappearing, as an hour before he had watched him and Wilson vanish down the passage together. He tapped his finger against his teeth, whistling to himself tunelessly and frowning. Then he climbed into bed and lighted a last cigarette.

5

IN the morning Christopher thought it must have been a dream, until he felt the knobbly bundle of shells under his pillow. Memory returned. His feet and ankles were scratched, and he remembered the brambles on the cliff path that had torn at them as he scrambled up it in the moonlight. He saw with surprise that he was wearing his green pyjamas, when surely it was the week for his blue and white pair.

Miss Norton came in to call the boys, as she always did when Matron was away. She walked over to him as he stood slowly unbuttoning his pyjama jacket, and fragments of what had happened in the night came back to him. He stared at her, unblinking, while she inspected him searchingly.

"All right, Wilson?" she asked then, briskly.

He nodded.

"Good. Hurry and dress, then," she said, and smiled at him. Then she went away down the dormitory, heels tapping on the polished boards. Christopher remembered the feel of the wood on his bare feet last night, and the cold chill of the tiled passage. He remembered running over the headland back to school, carrying the shells. Once he had tripped and fallen headlong in the short, damp grass; he had tripped too, coming upstairs, but Mr. Farquhar had been there then. He looked at his left shin; a big, black bruise decorated the skin. Christopher remembered with sharp alarm the moment when he had opened the garden door and found Mr. Farquhar standing behind it. Whatever would happen to him? The full horror and enormity of what he had done swept over him. For a moment he thought of running away, but first he must see about the shells. As soon as the bell went to allow the boys downstairs he hurried to Miss Wayne's music room and emptied them from his handkerchief on to the piano. Then it was time for breakfast and he was herded into the dining-room without a chance to escape.

Peter had spent a wakeful night, and rose full of a sense of his own inadequacy.

He glanced at Christopher during the meal, and saw that he seemed to be eating very little. Phyllis, looking as unperturbed as usual, leaned from her place at the end of the table and spoke to him.

Poor little blighter, he must be in hell, wondering what will happen to him, thought Peter, and remembered what Jennifer had said about the children going through their own private purgatories. Most of the ninety-nine other boys seemed very carefree, and preoccupied with consuming large amounts of bacon and tomato. "I must sort him out as soon as possible," Peter resolved, and when breakfast was over he instructed Christopher to come to his study before the bell went for prayers.

Dick Butler saw Peter cross the dining-room to speak to Christopher, and raised his ginger eyebrows.

Christopher thought again about running away after breakfast, but there were too many people about, and where could he run to? Instead he waited outside Peter's study until the master appeared, walking briskly down the passage towards him; then he stood up very straight, unaware that his teeth were chattering again.

Peter bundled him into the study and closed the door. Then he stood, looking at him, for a moment. The top of Christopher's head was on a level with the middle button of his own jacket. He was indeed a very little boy, and Peter saw the trembling lips.

"It's all right, Wilson, I'm not going to eat you," he said, and sat down, thus making it possible for the miscreant to meet his eyes without getting a crick in his neck.

"Now, suppose you tell me all about it?" he suggested.

Christopher stood before him and clenched his fingers.

"I—er—I," he began, and faltered into silence.

"How are you feeling this morning? You haven't got a headache, have you?" asked Peter.

"Oh, no, sir, I'm quite all right," Christopher assured him.

Peter saw that he was shaking. He sent up an urgent prayer for help and inspiration.

"You do remember going out of school last night?" he prompted.

Christopher nodded and gulped.

"It was to get the shells, Miss Wayne's shells," he managed to say.

A memory came to Peter. He recalled Jennifer taking Christopher back to school on the day of the water funk episode. "You collected them for her on the beach?" he tried.

"Yes. She helped, the day I—when I—" Christopher's voice trailed away again.

"The last time there was swimming?"

Christopher nodded.

Peter looked at him encouragingly. "Go on," he said.

"She put me in the choir. And we forgot the shells. She said it was a pity," burst out Christopher.

"You wanted to get the shells for Miss Wayne because she put you in the choir?" asked Peter.

"Yes, sir." Christopher gazed back at him unwaveringly across the desk, eyes large in his small, pale face.

"You're glad to be in the choir?"

"Yes, sir," said Christopher.

"I see. So you went to fetch the shells because you thought it would please Miss Wayne?" Peter felt like Sherlock Holmes.

"Yes, sir." Relief at being understood swamped Christopher.

"But you knew it was wrong to go out of school at night, didn't you?" asked Peter.

"Yes, sir. But it was the middle of the night, and I didn't think anyone would know," he said, hanging his head.

"That doesn't make it any better," said Peter firmly. "Rules are made to be obeyed, and most of them are for your own good and safety. You're quite old enough to understand that, Wilson."

"Yes, sir," mumbled Christopher.

Peter cogitated; how could he deal with this very small criminal? For a moment he contemplated suspending him from the choir, but at once he dismissed the idea of such a humiliating and long drawn-out punishment—besides, what would Jennifer say? Then inspiration came to him.

"Wilson," he said. "Do you remember we talked about being brave the other day?"

Christopher nodded.

"You were scared last night, weren't you, going out of school by yourself in the dark?"

"Yes, I was, sir," said Christopher feelingly.

"But you went, because you'd made up your mind to get the shells for Miss Wayne?"

"Yes, sir."

"Then you were very brave, Wilson." Peter looked at the little boy intently as he said this.

"You were brave," repeated Peter. "But you were also very, very naughty, and you must be punished."

"Yes, sir." Christopher's voice went flat.

"Six of the best, Wilson," said Peter resolutely, before his own determination failed.

Hope filled Christopher.

"You mean—you won't tell my mother?" he asked.

"I won't," said Peter. "No one else need know about it, unless you tell them." Here was not the type of boy to seek prestige by bragging of his punishment. Peter got up and went to the cupboard where the

100

cane, which only he and Geoffrey ever used, was kept. He took it out and tapped it against his fingers. Christopher's hands flew automatically to his small behind. Then he looked up at Peter and grinned.

"I'll just have to be brave again, won't I, sir?" he said.

It was raining. In the common-room the air was hazy with cigarette smoke, and steam from cups of tea. Most of the staff, except those on duty, were gathered there as usual after lunch.

"What's the big production going to be, Peter," asked Wilfrid Fitzgibbon. "Have you decided yet?"

Peter was leaning on the window-sill, gazing at the rain which poured in a deluge down the glass.

"Henry IV, part one," he said promptly.

"With girls?" asked Wilfrid.

"With certainly Lady Percy," said Peter with a grin. "Phyllis, we'll want all your powers of invention on the wardrobe problems."

Phyllis smiled. "The dresses will fall

apart if we use them many more times," she said.

"Don't you hire?" asked Dick Butler in surprised tones. He was sitting in the most comfortable armchair, intermittently flicking cigarette ash on the floor. His bright red hair was well smarmed down with some new hair oil he had been trying.

"We've got so many good things in the acting cupboard that we find we can usually manage," said Peter, trying to sound pleasant. Dick had only to open his mouth to be irritating; his whole attitude was off-hand and condescending towards his superiors and Peter had got to a stage of disliking him where he almost looked for offence, a rare state in him, for he was usually even-tempered.

"I should have thought it would have saved a lot of trouble to hire," said Dick, persisting.

"It would be expensive," said Peter shortly. Probably the boy was only seeking for information and his own critical attitude was unwarranted.

Every summer on Parents' Day a short concert and small play was given, usually a few scenes from Shakespeare which it was found impressed the parents. Peter was always in charge of these dramatic productions.

Ronald said, "How do you manage the lighting? Or do you do it out of doors?"

"Too chancy," said Peter. "We fry them in the gym. We've got some proper flats—we give it quite a professional touch."

Ronald's face was bright with interest. "Jolly good," he said enthusiastically.

"Like to help?" asked Peter. "I could do with some more assistance."

"Whether you want to or not, you're sure to be roped in, Ronald," said Phyllis with a smile. "Watch out."

Ronald grinned. "I enjoy that sort of thing," he said. "I've done quite a bit of it. Count me in, Peter."

"Who are you casting as Hotspur?" asked Wilfrid, who had been watching the two new masters' very different reactions with some amusement.

"Why, Pollock, of course, who else?" said Peter.

"He's a natural," said Ronald, "that swagger!"

"He gets very nervous," said Peter.

"You'd be surprised. It humbles him no end. Bradley for Lady Percy, of course, with those large blue saucer eyes."

"Will they ever learn their words?" wondered Ronald. Peter, making a huge effort to stop calling him Butler. "Then they've got them for life."

"Do they like doing Shakespeare?" asked Jennifer. "I should have thought they were too young."

"I don't think they are," said Peter. "It isn't any good trying any airy fairy stuff— Ariel is out, for instance, and Puck was very unpopular—but they like Falstaff and battle scenes. We stick to the histories, mostly."

"Why not Macbeth? Plenty of good murders in that," said Ronald, looking bloodthirsty.

"We did it last year," said Peter. "We must leave it for a year or two now. It went well. We sliced out a good deal of Lady Macbeth."

"Thank goodness," murmured Phyllis to Jennifer, who was sitting beside her on the sofa.

Wilfrid said, "Well, when you want my inspired help, Peter, let me know." He too looked out of the window. "Look at this rain; it will wash everything out of the ground," he grumbled. Muttering under his breath, he began to collect up his papers.

"Would you like to help with the play, Dick?" asked Peter, making a huge effort to stop calling him Butler.

Dick looked at him and hesitated.

"I'll be glad if you would, but it's only fair to warn you that it will take up a good deal of free time," Peter went on.

"I'll help, of course," said Dick, but his tone was surly.

Peter raised an eyebrow. Phyllis watched them; there was no doubt that they disliked one another. She could not understand why Dick had "taken against" Peter; his antipathy towards the younger man was more understandable, for Dick had an ungracious manner which in her charity Phyllis attributed to his extreme youth.

Wilfrid said, "We'll all be involved before the end. I try and keep out till the last moment; then, when everyone else's critical faculties are stale I come in, and with a touch of genius revolutionise the whole production. Peter then takes all the credit." He tucked the pile of books under his arm, and crossed the room. "My day to ring the bell," he said. "All in, obviously."

Peter nodded. "It looks like raining for ever," he said gloomily.

If it was too wet for the boys to go out they played noisy games in the school buildings, cricket in the long passage with a soft ball, sardines, and running games in the gym. Several days of wet weather, however, resulted in too much pent up high spirits among the boys, and frayed tempers among the staff.

One by one everyone drifted out of the common-room until only Phyllis and Jennifer were left.

"How depressing," said the girl, moving to the window where Peter had been and looking out. Even the cliff edge was hidden in the haze of sweeping rain. "Who would think it was May? It might be November."

"Grim," said Phyllis, "and cold too. What are you doing this afternoon, Jenny?"

"I think I'll really get down to working

out some ideas for the concert," said Jennifer. "I'm quite alarmed about it."

"Don't be," said Phyllis. "The parents have long ago given up expecting much. After all, the talent is limited as well as the repertoire."

Jennifer laughed. "It's easy to be calm at this distance, but I should think it will get nerve-wracking nearer the date," she said. "When is it to be, do we know?"

"Oh, at the end of June," said Phyllis. "I think Geoffrey makes a mistake, actually, in having it in the summer. It should be in the autumn. The boys are better running wild this term."

"Hm, yes. But I suppose it's tradition to have a 'do' in the summer, isn't it?" Jennifer said. "It doesn't give them long to learn their parts, does it?"

"Peter thinks if they have too long they get stale," answered Phyllis. "Four weeks' concentration is about right, he finds. There's no one in it who's got Common Entrance to worry about, so they can get down to it in earnest. He's got all the lighting and so on worked out systematically, and we've accumulated a good deal of battlement and castle scenery over the years. It's quite like a military operation now. Wilfrid always weighs in with the polishing touches. He has a very good eye for effect, and as he's a bit deaf he can pick out those who don't speak up. I expect Ronald will be a great help this year."

"I wonder how his novel's getting on," said Jennifer.

"I'm afraid to ask him in case he expects me to read it," said Phyllis. "I'm sure it's morbid."

"It might be very good," said Jennifer.

"Do you think he's an angry young man?" asked Phyllis.

"No," said Jennifer, laughing. "Dick's the angry one, but he doesn't seem to write."

"He isn't a cricketer—perhaps that's what makes him so bad-tempered," said Phyllis. "I've often noticed it. People who are bored with cricket but keen on rugger are like bears with sore heads in the summer. Probably he'll buck up next term."

She got up and began to collect the empty cups and saucers which stood about the room. Jennifer rose to help her.

"You like it here, don't you, Jennifer?" Phyllis asked her, frowning at a messy saucer where a cigarette stub lay in squalid saturation. "Ugh, isn't smoking a vile habit? Why don't I give it up? Look what these people do. Dick, I suppose."

"How foul," said Jennifer. "Yes, I do, Phyllis. I feel as if I've been here for ages, already. Everyone's been so kind and friendly."

"We like having you," said Phyllis. "Your predecessor had a moustache and halitosis, and no talent."

Jennifer laughed. Phyllis thought how pretty she was, and how charming in her moments of gaiety; no wonder Peter had been so swiftly bowled over.

They piled the crockery tidily on the tray, and dallied, reluctant to leave the cosy, warm, but smoke-filled room. Phyllis pulled one of the windows down a few inches; some rain scurried in, but some smoke also went out.

"How long have you been here, Phyllis?" asked Jennifer curiously.

"Fifteen years," said Phyllis. "I'm the oldest inhabitant, except for Wilfrid."

"Have you never wanted to go anywhere else?" Jennifer asked.

"Oh, a long time ago I thought about it vaguely," said Phyllis. "But one way and the other it came to nothing. I started as the most junior assistant matron, after I left school, and then I was head matron for a bit—that was in the war, when we couldn't get any SRNs who were sound in wind and limb; and then the secretary left so I began to deal with that; and then Marion wanted me to do the housekeeping."

"You're awfully vital to the general structure," said Jennifer. "You understand it all." She reflected in astonishment that Phyllis had known no other adult life than that at Arrowhurst.

"I'm not really," said Phyllis with a smile. "I'm good at making myself look busy, so that Geoffrey will think I'm indispensable. Actually, Marion and a typist could easily do what I do."

Yes, two people, thought Jennifer. Aloud, she said, "Oh, it isn't your work so much, it's you. Everyone depends on you. 'Ask Phyllis' is the answer to all questions."

Phyllis laughed, but she looked pleased. "Well, don't expect me to draft your music programme," she said, "for I hope this year we'll get away from 'Scotland the Brave' and 'The Lord's my Shepherd', followed by Beethoven's Minuet in G played by a Jones."

"Chopin this time," said Jennifer, "and a Bach chorale sung solo by Wilson, followed by excerpts from 'The Mikado.'"

6

"LOOK at this, my dear. We are to be highly privileged." Geoffrey handed Marion a letter written in flowing handwriting upon purple deckle-edged paper.

"What is it?" Marion took the letter from him and carried it to the window as she read. "Gracious, what a bore," she said, when she had reached the flourishing signature.

"That's hardly the way to refer to our most celebrated mother," said Geoffrey with a smile. "All the same, I could do without a visit from her myself." He sighed and picked up another letter from the pile that waited for attention on his desk.

"Well, perhaps it's a good thing," said Marion. "Phyllis says she never writes to the child, and he's such a pale, pathetic little fellow. It may cheer him up to see her."

"Wilson isn't pale and pathetic any

longer," said Geoffrey. "You can't have seen him lately. He's changed completely. Peter seems to think it's because he's in the choir—it's given him a bit of prestige. He's learning to swim, and he's even made a few runs at cricket—and I hear he's third in form this week."

"Oh, good. He must have settled down at last." Marion helped herself to a cigarette from the shagreen box on Geoffrey's desk. "Well, let's hope his mother doesn't unsettle him again. What a nuisance the woman is, wanting to come to tea. I shall have to cancel my hair-do, I suppose."

"I shouldn't—let Phyl look after her," said Geoffrey absently, reading another letter.

Marion regarded him with a half-smile.

"And leave you to be vamped by the pair of them?" she said lightly. "No, I'll change my appointment to the morning, then I'll feel equal to coping with Janine." She came up behind Geoffrey's chair and put her hands on his shoulders for a moment. "Never let it be said that I shirked my duty," she said, turning away from him again. Her tone was flippant, but her face was serious as she watched him.

113

He was working methodically through his post, frowning to himself. He looked tired, and she wondered again how well he really was. She made a little face to herself; he had not been listening to her. Her words were unimportant, but sometimes she wondered if he would notice if she were to say she was leaving him. He would probably only say, "Nonsense, dear, of course you don't mean that," and go on reading, his mind already busy with classics for the Sixth Form. She turned away and went back to the window, where she leaned on the sill and watched him in an unusually critical mood. His body was as familiar to her as her own, but she wondered how much of his mind she knew. She was aware that she lacked the intellectual capacity to be his perfect companion, and that much of the success of their marriage was owed to her social sense, which kept the staff happy and free from serious quarrels among themselves, and which was invaluable when dealing with the parents. In her franker moments of self-examination she knew herself too unsubtle and materialistic to follow Geoffrey among his highest aims. If they had never met, she supposed in time he would have drifted into marrying Phyllis. Would he have been happier? "Let Phyl look after her," he had said about Janine Dufay. How seriously had he meant it? How much did he still rely on Phyllis? A rare mood of jealousy came upon Marion, but at once she felt both ashamed and contemptuous. Phyllis, good, worthy soul, could never compete with herself for looks or poise, even if she did know all that there was to know about scrubby little boys. Marion looked at the well-shaped back of Geoffrey's greying head, and felt a wild frustration because she would never know or understand all that went on inside it. As though to assert her rights in him she moved swiftly up behind his chair again, and bending, pressed her well-cared-for cheek against his hair.

"Darling, don't worry about Janine. I'll see we have a splendid tea, and I'll wear my best dress to impress her," she said, and kissed him fiercely. Then she walked quickly out of the room.

Geoffrey watched her go with a smile of tolerant affection. Of course she would, as always, deal perfectly with the visiting mother, he needed no reassurance about that. She was seldom demonstrative, and he wondered for a moment what had provoked this small display. Then his mind returned to the impossibility of getting Tompkins to construe a single line of Greek, and the letter in his hand from General Tompkins confidently expecting a classical scholarship to a leading public school.

There was a match that afternoon. It was very hot, and the field shimmered in the bright sunlight. The boys watching were quieter than usual, too hot to wrangle much, and content to pay attention to the game. Peter, Phyllis and Jennifer were sitting on a bench under a big oak tree, glad to be taking no more energetic part in the afternoon's activities. Phyllis was feeling that she was a gooseberry, and was trying to summon the energy to rise and leave the other two.

"I hear Wilson's mother is coming to tea tomorrow," said Jennifer idly.

"Oh, is she? I didn't know," said Peter.

"Yes, she's in a play that's opening in Brighampton this week, so she decided to come over," said Phyllis. "What an honour for us," she added, with some malice.

"Wilson's on top of the world about it," said Jennifer. "He told everyone in singing this morning. How he has come on lately!"

Phyllis and Peter exchanged a glance.

"I'm still wondering how he got those shells," Jennifer continued. "You know, Peter, I told you I found a whole lot of shells on the piano one morning about ten days ago, and they were just like the ones he and I collected on the beach and then left behind. There was a particular one, unusually marked, that I remembered. But the boys weren't swimming last week, so how could he have fetched them?"

"I think we'll have to tell her, Phyl," said Peter with a grin. "She'll only keep on about it if we don't, and worm it out of the boy himself in the end."

Jennifer threw a dandelion head at him.

"What grisly secret are you hiding?" she asked laughing. "Out with it."

"Wilson made a midnight pilgrimage down the cliff to get the shells, in gratitude for being put in the choir," said Peter.

"Midnight! No!" Jennifer's grey eyes opened wide in horrified astonishment.

"Well, eleven o'clock," Peter qualified.

"But how?" Jennifer stared at him.

"I caught him coming in at the garden door. It was Monday of last week. Do you remember, Jenny? I'd just left you at the lodge."

A quick glance of understanding passed between them, and Phyllis, seeing it, suddenly felt very middle-aged and lonely.

"Yes, I remember." Jennifer coloured slightly. "Go on."

"You'd evidently said something about it being a pity they were left on the path, and he thought as the weather was bad and there was no bathing he'd make a special trip to fetch them for you. He walked straight into me on the way back," said Peter.

"But how awful!" gasped Jennifer. "Just think of him going all that way alone in the dark! He must have been scared stiff. He's not one of the ones with no nerves."

"He *was* scared," said Peter grimly. "So was I. I never thought any of them would get out at night."

"Peter prowls round every night now at eleven to see all the bolts are still shut," said Phyllis. She did not add that she too had been up in the small hours several times, thinking she had heard a noise, and had gone round all the dormitories to make sure no one was missing.

"What did you do?" asked Jennifer.

"Phyl dealt with him. Thank goodness she was awake," said Peter.

"We had quite a time, Jennifer," said Phyllis. "Cups of tea in the surgery. It was the night Matron was away—perhaps luckily."

"But how awful!" Jennifer exclaimed. "Why, he might have fallen down the cliff in the dark!"

"I know, but he didn't. There was a moon, you remember." Peter looked at her with great tenderness. "It doesn't do to think too much of what might have happened. Luckily it all ended well."

Jennifer said slowly, "But it's since then that he's bucked up so much. He's cheerful now, and even noisy. Why?"

"Because Peter caned him," said Phyllis bluntly.

"You didn't!" Jennifer looked horrified.

119

Peter stared at the grass. "I still don't know if it was right," he muttered.

"It was perfectly right," Phyllis told him firmly. "He had to have some sort of punishment, and that was over at once, not like doing without sweets or writing lines, and no one knew about it. Children understand justice, Jennifer, even rough justice. Wilson knew he'd been naughty; he would have thought it very odd not to have been punished."

"I thought I'd probably given him a complex for life," said Peter, looking sheepish.

"How could you beat him?" asked Jennifer. "That pathetic little boy!"

Phyllis observed, "I expect it was the most difficult beating Peter's ever given." She looked at Jennifer. "I doubt if it was a hard one, and the child understood. You must judge by results, my dear."

Peter said, "I think he's changed because he's discovered himself capable of courage. I told him he'd shown courage in going down for the shells."

A glimmer of comprehension came to Jennifer. Dimly she perceived the intuitive wisdom, something quite apart from experience, that was one of the qualities which distinguished Peter from most of the other masters.

"And he's found he can deal with his homesickness too," she said slowly.

"Putting him in the choir is what really started it," said Peter. "He's found there's something he can do really well, and now he's trying hard at everything, but with confidence, not hopelessly, like he used to. Nothing breeds success like success. He's being very plucky in the sea. If the weather holds and it stays calm he'll swim quite soon. I wish some of the others possessed his powers of application."

"Poor little boy," said Jennifer. "I wonder what his mother is really like." She remembered the hard, closed look that had come over Christopher's face when she suggested that he might ask his mother to let him learn the piano.

"Well, we'll soon know," said Phyllis, getting up. "Marion's ordered a ritzy tea for her. It's red carpet to the fore tomorrow." She dusted her hands on her gingham skirt. "It's much too hot outside," she said. "I'm going indoors," and she walked away from them over the field. In a moment a group of boys had run up to waylay her and talk to her.

"How nice she is, and how wise," said Jennifer, watching her.

"Yes." Peter was looking at Jennifer and not at the departing Phyllis.

"Does this sort of thing often happen? Boys getting out, I mean?" Jennifer asked.

"Hardly ever," Peter said. "A boy disappeared about a year ago, but he only got as far as Charnton. He'd got his school cap on, and the baker spotted him and brought him back. He'd done it for a dare, little devil. Thank goodness that's the only other time I've known it happen."

"It is a responsibility, isn't it? All those other people's children," said Jennifer.

"It's an opportunity," said Peter. "It's very rewarding to find a boy who likes to be taught, or to help a mother's darling learn to stand on his own feet."

"They don't seem very mother's-darling-ish, on the whole," said Jennifer.

"I think they're tougher than our generation," said Peter. "No nannies, or very few, and not much money in most cases. Of course, we grew up in the war, which ought to have hardened us up; but these boys have mostly had to do much more for themselves. We only get a few now who can't tie up their own shoes or dress themselves."

"Do you mean to say people let their sons go away without making sure they can look after themselves?" Jennifer was amazed.

"You'd be surprised," said Peter. "I don't suppose the parents have a clue what a give-away the boys are about how they've been brought up."

Jennifer was silent. She looked at the players on the field. Ronald Cross and a visiting master, umpiring, looked like giants among the pigmies surrounded by the teams.

"One of them might play in a Test Match one day," she said.

"One might be Prime Minister," said Peter, "or the first man to land on the moon."

"That's how Mr. Frost thinks, isn't it?" said Jennifer. "Expecting the miracle, I mean."

"It's the only way to think," said Peter. "Expect the best, I mean, from every boy, and you'll probably get it in the end, though the potential bests of every boy vary fantastically."

"But aren't there boys who won't produce their best?" she asked.

"If they fail, it's our failure too," he said. "We do get some."

"I see." Jennifer pondered this. A dark curl fell across the pale skin of her cheek, and Peter longed to touch it. She seemed a little remote this afternoon; sometimes he felt that she withdrew herself from him, but at other times he was sure he knew just what she was thinking or feeling, and that she understood his mind too. He hoped ardently that the moments of remoteness would diminish, until there was between them an invisible bond of perfect sympathy, when no barrier remained.

"Sir! Sir! Please, sir!" Christopher hopped on one leg in front of Peter in the passage, while round them a stream of boys made their devious ways to their form-rooms, some swooping with arms outstretched as jet bombers, some growling under Maserati engines driven by Stirling Moss,

124

some wrangling and pushing, very few simply walking.

"Yes, Wilson, what is it?" Peter stopped, his arms full of books, looking down at the eager little boy.

"Please, sir, my mother's coming to tea today, did you know?" he asked.

"Yes, I did, Wilson," said Peter. "How nice."

"I had a letter," said Christopher proudly. "Look!"

Peter duly admired the large purple envelope, and thought of the regular, faithful letters written by the ninety-nine other mothers.

"She's too busy to write much," Christopher was explaining. "She's a famous actress you know. She would write to me every week if she had time, that's what she'd like to do," he declared defiantly.

"Yes, I'm sure she would, Wilson," said Peter. "Well, you'll be seeing her today. That will be good, won't it?"

"Oh yes," said Christopher. "What a pity I can't swim yet. She could have seen me."

"You'll be able to by the end of term,"

said Peter. "She can see you swimming in the holidays."

"Yes, I suppose so." Christopher looked worried for a moment. The holidays were still on a far horizon, unplanned for as unseen. He pushed the thought of them away, and basked in the joy of today. "Oh well," he said, and grinned, and ran off.

Peter raised his eyebrows, continuing on down the passage towards his form-room. Funny little fellow, he thought, with a smile. Well, at last he seemed to be settling, and that was a lucky result of what could have been a tragedy.

Janine Dufay Wilson arrived at twenty-minutes to five, having said she planned to come at four. Marion was seething, since she had been waiting in idleness for forty minutes and had needlessly upset her entire afternoon's arrangements. But she sailed gracefully over the parquet floor of the hall to meet the guest, hand out-stretched in welcome, as though she had expected her only at that minute.

Janine was tiny. Marion felt absurdly glad of her height as she looked down upon the perfect little creature who approached. Each blonde curl was in its appointed position, each eyelash stood separated from its fellow in a stiff fence round the big blue eyes.

She's like a doll, thought Marion, shaking hands.

She led the way into her drawing-room, sure that the visitor must be impressed by the valuable carpets and old furniture. Long windows, framed with heavy green brocade curtains, opened on to the garden, and the air was full of the scent of flowers. A large vase of roses and delphiniums, beautifully arranged, stood on a wigstand in a corner, and another, containing lupins, filled the fireplace.

"Do sit down, Mrs. Wilson," said Marion, wondering too late if she should have said "Miss Dufay." She indicated the sofa. "My husband will be here soon, he's busy with the boys at the moment." Geoffrey had in fact waited for Janine until half-past four, when his patience ran out and he made off in the direction of the lower field.

Janine did not enjoy female company at any time, but today she saw herself in the role of dainty mother, too youthful to own a schoolboy son, and she fluttered with her tea cup while Marion asked about the new play.

"It's a lovely part," cooed Janine, "And we seem to have made a success in the provinces. We open in London next month." She did not say that she had only got the part because the original leading lady had fallen ill, and the producer's next three choices, all younger actresses than she, had turned it down. She talked happily about the play, and described all her dresses for each act, while Marion ate a cucumber sandwich. Finally the two ladies decided that honour in regard to the food was satisfied. Marion rang for it to be removed, and simmered angrily to herself over the untouched chocolate cake; the tiresome little thing would be on a diet, she fumed, with the wrath of an unappreciated hostess.

"Shall we go outside? The boys are playing cricket," she said. "Christopher doesn't do much prep. yet, and we push the little ones out whenever it's fine. They're usually busy with a bat somewhere about." She led the way out of the french window, and over the lawn, and Janine on her stiletto heels walked beside her. Marion had considered whether Christopher should be invited to take tea in the drawing-room, but the boys had their "gab,"—a sort of snack tea, standing up—out of doors when fine, at four o'clock, and their high tea at six, so that she had decided to let him stick to his own time-table and be spared the possible social embarrassment of a dainty ladies' tea-party. Now, with Janine so late, she was glad she had done so.

They crossed the garden, and as they reached the lower field a group of boys carrying towels passed them, with Peter in their midst. Marion hailed him with relief. Parents did not often defeat her, but she could think of nothing to say to Janine, and felt in her she had met her Waterloo.

"This is Mr. Farquhar, our senior master," she said, detaching him.

"Oh, but we've met before, Mr. Farquhar," said Janine, looking up at Peter with her china blue eyes.

"Good God, did I really think she was pretty?" thought Peter to himself, aghast, whilst politely shaking hands. Aloud he said, "Why yes, indeed. How do you do?" Then, recollecting himself and smoothing his rumpled hair, "Please excuse my untidiness—we've been swimming."

"How brave of you, in all that cold sea," said Janine, as though addressing one who had navigated the waters of the Antarctic in a canoe. "Are you really the senior master? You don't look old enough," she added, waving her eyelashes at him.

To be told this was one of the crosses in Peter's life, but it was not usually accompanied by such a look. Over the top of her blonde head he and Marion exchanged an eloquent glance.

"Mr. Farquhar is older than he appears," said Marion.

"Christopher's getting on very well, Mrs. Wilson," Peter said quickly. "He'll soon be able to swim." He looked about him. Where on earth was the child? He'd been clearly visible on the field half an hour before. "He's somewhere about, I'll find him for you," he offered, preparing to escape. Under the actress's unwavering stare he felt like a mite beneath a microscope.

Janine put out a small hand to detain him. "Don't hurry away," she said. "Do tell me, Mr. Farquhar, what is it you teach?"

"English," said Peter flatly.

"Oh. Shakespeare, and all that?" said Janine.

"Er—yes. Grammar too," said Peter, ridiculously, "and history as well."

They began to walk across the field, Peter heading in the direction where he was sure Christopher and his confreres would be. Janine was tiny between Marion and the young man; she kept her eyes firmly fixed upon his face, and Marion might not have existed for all the notice that she took of her. Peter, in deep water, kept trying to retreat from her personal and leading remarks as they paced solemnly over the field, but Marion would not help him. He saw that she was almost helpless with laughter, and in spite of his embarrassed discomfort his opinion of her rose, for he had not previously held a high estimate of her sense of humour.

"You must come and see my new play," Janine finally decided. "I'll send you a ticket. I'm sure you can easily pop over to Brighampton. Come round and see me afterwards. You too, of course, Mrs.

Frost," she added tardily, "and your husband."

"How very kind," muttered Peter. "Now where is Christopher?"

At that moment Geoffrey appeared from round the corner of the house. He had been escaping, after one glance at Janine, in the opposite direction, when he had run into Phyllis who had sent him firmly back. Now he approached, reluctantly, and Marion waited in delight to see how Janine would deal with two men. Geoffrey looked very distinguished as he came towards them with his always slow, now slower still, long strides, his hands clasped behind his back.

"I'm afraid I was a little late for tea," said Janine when he reached them, trying to look like a malefacting fourth former. "I would have been sorry to miss you," she said.

"Er—yes. I'm sorry not to have been here when you arrived," said Geoffrey warily.

"Don't tell me you've been in the sea too," said Janine. "I think Mr. Farquhar is perfectly splendid. Just imagine, he's been swimming!" She opened her eyes very wide at Peter, and in that instant he ceased to be amused and was instead disgusted.

"No. Cricket," said Geoffrey briefly.

"Do *you* play?" asked Janine, and her glance took in the whole of Geoffrey. To Marion it was the rawest thing, and she waited to see her husband's reaction. His eyes hardened, and he looked at his watch.

"Not now," he said, and went on quickly, "I'm afraid you will have to excuse me, I have a class now, the scholarship boys. Mr. Farquhar here, my senior master, and my wife, will be delighted to show you round. Goodbye, Mrs. Wilson," and with a curt nod he departed.

A bell rang in the distance, and all the boys who were dotted about the field also began to run towards the house.

Janine, with a shrewd expression on her face, now also consulted her watch.

"Good gracious, just look at the time," she exclaimed. "It's all been so fascinating, I had no idea it was so late." She left no doubt about just what it was she found so fascinating as she fastened her eyes upon Peter. "I must fly, I'm afraid, or I'll be late for the show. It takes over an hour for me to dress and make-up, you see."

"But Christopher!" Peter cried.

"I don't see him about," said Janine, glancing perfunctorily round. "Give him my love. And remember, you're coming to my play. I'll be waiting to see you backstage."

"And you mean to say she never even spoke to the child?"

Peter and Jennifer were sitting on the shore on his jacket, and he had just finished describing Janine's visit. It was nine o'clock, and still warm; before them the sea shimmered like rich satin, with the little waves lapping on the sand. There was only a slight breeze, and Jennifer wore her blue cardigan loosely slung round her shoulders, over her pink cotton dress.

"Not a word," said Peter. "She stopped me from fetching him earlier. It seems he saw her—I went to look for him after she'd gone. He was watching from the corner of the field, and I hadn't spotted him. You know how alike they all are in the distance, and anyway I thought he'd come along if he saw her."

"But why did she come here at all?" asked Jennifer.

"Search me. To overwhelm us with sex appeal, I should think," said Peter. He shuddered. "Jenny, it was revolting. I thought it was funny at first, it was so barefaced, but when Geoff came and she set to work on him, too, and looked at him —I can't tell you what it was like! She's a frightful woman."

"How horrible," said Jennifer. She was quiet for a moment, and then she said, "Perhaps we should be sorry for her. She may be unhappy and lonely. Her marriage has gone wrong, after all."

"No wonder," said Peter grimly.

"That may be why she's like this," said Jennifer.

"She isn't normal—she's obscene," said Peter.

"Well, she's gone now," said Jennifer soothingly.

"Thank God," said Peter, taking deep breaths of sea air.

"Was Wilson very upset?" Jennifer asked.

"He went rather white. I thought it best not to say too much. I told him she'd been delayed on the way here, and could only stay a few minutes. Poor little chap, he just turned away and mooched off. He'd been so thrilled about her coming."

"What an awful person she must be," said Jennifer. "You'd think she'd be longing to see her son."

"Giving birth doesn't always make a mother," said Peter, bitterly. "Nor procreation a father. Don't let's talk about her any more, Jenny, it's too vile." He got up and held out a hand to help her to her feet.

"Let's walk for a bit, and get some clean air into our lungs," he said fiercely.

"All right."

Jennifer looked at him as they set off down the beach. He felt her gaze upon him, and turned his head to look down at her; he smiled then, a brief, absent-minded smile.

"Sorry, I'm not good company tonight," he said gruffly. Then he took her hand and tucked it through the crook of his arm, and held it there with his own.

The nightmare returned to Christopher that night. Again he heard his mother's voice, hard and high, and the dreadful words she had said; but in his dream the face of the man who was her companion became the face of Peter.

7

TWO days later Geoffrey received in the post three centre stalls tickets from Janine for her new play.

"Well, I'm certainly not going to that," he said at once, and was about to throw them into the waste-paper basket when Marion intervened.

"Give them to Peter," she said. "It's probably a good play, and he might like to take Jennifer. It would be a nice evening for them. They're quite serious, those two. I hope something will come of it."

"They're very young," said Geoffrey. "Why is it that women always want to marry off any couples that cast even a slightly curious eye at one another?" He handed her the tickets. "Here they are, if you think they'd enjoy it. Personally I wouldn't go to see that woman if you paid me a thousand pounds."

Marion laughed. "She was frightful," she agreed. "Still you didn't see much of her. Peter and I had the worst of it."

"Well, she left us in peace for a whole year without a visit, let's hope we can now be spared for another," said her husband, picking up the next letter from the heap. "Who do you recommend to be the odd man out? She's sent three tickets, I see. I thought young Cross was rather smitten with Jennifer."

"I think he is, in a resigned sort of way," said Marion. "He's years younger than she is. They went to a concert last week, I think Jennifer rather took pity on him and was bludgeoned into going."

"I hope she isn't going to break the hearts of all the staff," said Geoffrey mildly, putting a paper-knife under the flap of the envelope.

"It's a long time since we've had anyone so pretty or so nice here," said Marion. "Dick would like to make a pass at her, too, if he had the nerve."

"What a vulgar expression, 'make a pass,'" commented Geoffrey. "I thought he'd fallen for you, the young ones usually seem to."

This was true: many a very young man had walked miles out of his way round the playing field hoping for a kind look from

Marion's green eyes, until time had taught him that the assistant matrons were more readily available.

"Not Dick," said Marion. "I don't really like him, Geoff. Shall you keep him?"

"Well, I hadn't really thought about it," said Geoffrey. "He hasn't said he wants to leave. Why don't you like him? Because he has remained immune from your spell?"

"Brute," said Marion, laughing. "No, I don't know what it is. He's sinister, somehow. He slinks about in those sandals he wears, watching people all the time, and he doesn't join in with the others in the common-room. He looks so like a fox, too. I think he's rather moody, probably."

She said this with the air of one making a profound discovery.

"Aren't we all?" asked Geoffrey, absent-mindedly.

"You aren't," said Marion, watching him. Sometimes remote, and incomprehensible to her often, but never moody, she thought gratefully. "Can he teach?" she enquired.

"Who? Oh, Butler? Not very well. He likes laying down the law to the boys, and he's good with them at games although he doesn't like cricket. He'll do, for a term or two. Young Cross, though, is another matter. He's good. I'll be sorry when we lose him. Perhaps he'll come back to us after the Army's finished with him."

"Perhaps he won't have to go now," said Marion. "Thank goodness he's had his hair cut at last. He'll desert us to be a writer—he's busy scribbling in the library whenever he has a spare moment, did you know?"

Geoffrey nodded. "Plenty of schoolmasters write books in the holidays," he said, "keeps them out of mischief. Well, you do what you like with those tickets, my dear, as long as you don't expect me to go."

Marion shuffled them together in her hand. "I'll find a home for them," she promised.

On the night for which the theatre tickets had been sent Peter had a rehearsal for the school play, which he could not change. He had also been so revolted by Janine that like Geoffrey he felt no desire whatever to go and watch her perform. Jennifer, however, had never seen her act, and was curious; she and Phyllis decided to go together. At the last moment, because it was his half-day, they gave Dick Butler the third ticket.

"Then he'll drive us, and we shan't have to rush for the bus," said Phyllis, in a most mercenary way.

They rattled off along the coast road to Brighampton in Dick's old sports car, which was held together more by luck than bolts. He felt pleased at the prospect of spending an evening with Jennifer, right under the nose of Farquhar, as he put it to himself; but some of the pleasure of thus, as he thought, scoring off Peter, diminished when she climbed decisively into the back of his car, and thereby compelled Phyllis to sit in front with him.

All the way to Brighampton Dick showed off, roaring along in low gear with a lot of noise up the hills, and doing a great deal of loud double-declutching and revving. Jennifer felt slightly sick as they swerved along the road, rushing in and out among the traffic in what seemed a very reckless way for any car, let alone such an old and dubious one. Phyllis, in front, seemed to be seated directly on top of the road surface, and could barely see out of the windscreen, for she was small, and there were no springs left in the sagging passenger seat. She closed her eyes when she found, as they climbed a hill, that all she could see was the sky, and did not open them again until the engine was switched off.

They were not able to park near the theatre: it was drizzling, and blowing hard, but Dick, devoid of chivalry, did not deliver them to the door and then go himself to dispose of the car; instead he parked in a side street a few hundred yards away, leaving them to brave the weather on their feet.

"Ugh, how horrid," said Phyllis, stepping out of the car into a puddle. "What a beastly evening."

Dick did not think of coming round to help the ladies descend.

"Where did he go to school?" muttered Phyllis crossly, shaking herself; Jennifer's slim legs appeared from the back of the car, as she unwedged herself with difficulty from her cramped position in the small space where she had been sitting. "Mind the puddle."

Dick stood impatiently waiting for them, then commanded that they should lock the car door. He made much play with locking the one on his side.

"Silly ass, can't he see anyone can get in through the cracks," grumbled Phyllis. "Come on, we'll be late," she added, setting off down the road at a brisk pace. Jennifer, who was tying a scarf round her head to stop her hair getting wet in the rain, hastened after her. "We shouldn't criticise a free ride, it's too ungrateful," she said, laughing. Dick was left behind, still fiddling with the doors. "Shouldn't we wait for him?"

"Beastly boy, he's got no manners," said Phyllis.

"Ssh, he'll hear you," said Jennifer, looking round to see if he was coming.

"I don't care," said Phyllis. "I don't know when I've had such a frightful journey."

"Well, you thought it would be better than the bus, remember," Jennifer pointed out, still laughing.

"I was wrong," said Phyllis.

Dick, forced to run to overtake them, now caught up, and the three strode along the front and then turned down the road to the theatre. The wind blew gustily after them, and the rain showered down their backs as they joined the crowd entering the theatre. Inside, it was warm and rather stifling. The lights were already going down as they found their seats, and a hush came over the audience. The curtain rose to reveal a typical drawing-room set, and the play began. It was a murder story, with the action taking place in a country house where the usual group of improbable guests were simultaneously staying, all with plenty of motives for murdering each other. It was a tightly-written plot that allowed little licence to the cast, and only a very incompetent actor could fail to give an adequate performance. Janine looked suitably fragile and appealing as the young bride of suspect number one.

"I say, isn't Janine good?" said Dick with enthusiastic familiarity at the end of the first act. "Pretty, too, isn't she? What a looker!" He clicked his tongue in appreciation. Jennifer winced.

"Why don't you go round and see her?" said Phyllis naughtily.

"Do you think I could?" Dick looked

astonished. His red hair seemed to bristle on his head with excitement at the idea.

"Why not? She gave us the tickets, after all," said Phyllis.

"We'll all go," said Dick, but his face fell at the thought.

"I'd rather not," said Phyllis comfortably. "I'm too lazy to disturb myself. But take Jenny with you, by all means."

"No, I'll stay, if you don't mind, Dick," said Jennifer. She was reluctant to meet Janine face to face and be beholden to her, in however small a way.

"How do I do it?" asked Dick, losing confidence.

"Send a note round. Ask one of the attendants to have it delivered. Suggest going round in the second interval," said Phyllis firmly, as if quite accustomed to haunting stage doors.

"Righto." Dick was keen now. He searched in his pocket and found a notebook from which he tore a page, and scribbled busily with a green ballpoint pen. "I'm saying Mr. Frost couldn't come and sent me in his place, in case she wonders," he explained.

"Very wise," said Phyllis, winking at Jennifer.

Dick went off and gave his note to one of the attendants. The curtain had risen on the second act before an answer came, and was passed along the row of seats with mutters of annoyance from the occupants. Then Dick caused more disturbance by lighting his cigarette-lighter with many frustrated clicks in order to read the note by its flame.

"She's asked me round," he said in a noisy whisper.

Jennifer smiled and nodded, meanwhile trying to listen to what was being said on the stage above his clatter. Dick then settled back in his seat again, to the relief of his neighbours, and became absorbed once more in the play.

Act Two was passed in casting suspicion in turn on every member of the cast still left alive, even Janine, who had plenty of opportunities for displaying her histrionic talent when being questioned by the detective. Her performance was good, though possibly a more subtle actress would have been able to add dimension to the character. Dick stared at her as though fascinated all the time she was on the stage, and he was out of his seat like a shot from a gun when the curtain fell.

"I'm not sure we ought to let him go round there by himself, if she's really as bad as Peter says," said Jennifer doubtfully. "He isn't very old."

"Don't be silly, Jenny. That young man can take care of himself if anyone can," said Phyllis.

"It's all on the top really," said Jennifer. "I don't think he's a bit sure of himself underneath, that's what makes him so bumptious."

Phyllis was not listening. "He's so boring, I felt we must get rid of him for a bit," she said. "Let's go and look for some coffee."

Jennifer shrugged and obediently followed Phyllis out of the auditorium. When they had acquired cups of coffee by standing in a patient queue, Phyllis, reinvigorated, said cheerfully, "It won't do Dick any harm to singe his wings a bit. I'm all for the odd wild oat."

Jennifer could not help wondering how wild an oat Phyllis meant. The world of Arrowhurst was so sheltered and its turmoils all of little stature; what did Phyllis, who had only known that world, understand about the wider one outside?

"Janine doesn't care one rap for her son," went on Phyllis. "That much is certain. Poor little boy, I can't think why she bothered to come down at all the other day, if she didn't want to speak to him."

Jennifer decided not to quote what Peter had said.

"She's pretty, isn't she, in an artificial sort of way, don't you think?" she said. "I suppose it's difficult, when she's acting at night and presumably has to sleep and rehearse by day, to look after the child."

"Other people do it. It may be difficult, but it isn't impossible," said Phyllis. "It's a great pity the boy can't continue to live with his grandmother. She's a dear old lady, it was she who came down to see the school and who made all the arrangements for Wilson, years ago. She had a stroke some time back and she's pretty much of an invalid now."

"Does his mother never come to take him out?" asked Jennifer.

"She never has," Phyllis replied. "I think Jones II is taking him out on

Sunday, so that will be one outing for him."

"How sad it is," said Jennifer.

"Well, we can't do anything about it, except try to get him toughened up a bit so that he can cope," said Phyllis briskly. "Now, who do you think did the murder?"

They talked about the play until the bell rang for the end of the interval. Dick had not returned when they went back to their seats.

"How I dread the drive back," said Phyllis. "It'll be pouring harder than ever by then, and that wretched little car leaks like a sieve."

"It was your idea to ask Dick," said Jennifer.

"Well, everyone else was either too busy or hadn't got a car," said Phyllis.

"We needn't do it again," said Jennifer soothingly.

Dick returned as the curtain rose, flushed and grinning, with even the tips of his ears red. He trod on a row of toes as he stumbled back to his seat, and did not glance at his companions as Janine came on to the stage for her last entrance.

The murderer duly met retribution by falling over a cliff while pursuing another victim, and the play ended.

Dick said, blushing furiously, as they came out of the theatre doors on to the steps leading to the path, "Phyllis, I wonder, if I take you down to the bus station, whether you'd mind going back on the bus. Miss Dufay has—er—asked me to supper."

"Well!" Phyllis thought of protesting; then she remembered all her complaints about the journey in.

"Of course, I'll drive you back if you like," Dick said reluctantly. He felt very excited. He could not know that Janine's latest lover had just flown off to Hollywood, so that she was bored and would grasp any opportunity for diversion; he was only aware that Marion, Jennifer, and the others at school considered him young and callow, whereas Janine clearly did not find this to his disadvantage.

"Why, there's Peter," cried Jennifer, hurrying down the steps.

Peter's green Morris Minor was parked by the kerb, and he stood beside it, anxiously scanning the faces of the emerging audience. He saw them as she spoke and went quickly to meet them.

"Hullo, I came to take you back," he said.

"Oh Peter, how kind of you, but we came with Dick," said Jennifer.

"Oh, I didn't realise that," said Peter. "I thought you'd come on the bus."

"Dick has another engagement now," said Phyllis firmly. "Thank you so much for bringing us in, Dick. Goodbye." She marched towards Peter's car with thankful steps.

"Oh—goodbye," said Dick, unable to believe his luck. He hurried off, before it could be changed, even forgetting his dislike of Peter as he hastened round to the back of the stage.

Phyllis got into the rear seat of the car, deaf to Jennifer's half-hearted suggestions that she should sit in front, and Peter shut the doors upon them and got into his own seat.

"Did you enjoy the play?" he asked.

They told him about it, and Phyllis described, with much exaggeration, the horrors of their journey in Dick's car.

"I hope he wasn't offended at my

sweeping you off from under his nose. He's so touchy, that fellow," said Peter. "Must come of having red hair."

"I don't care if he was, I'm thankful not to have to go with him," said Phyllis. "Anyway, he was trying to get rid of us on to the bus. Mrs. Wilson has invited him to supper."

Jennifer looked startled. She had not heard all that Dick said.

"I suppose he knows what he's doing," said Peter, "I doubt if Mrs. Wilson would respect his lack of years."

"I shouldn't worry," said Phyllis comfortably. "How did your Barding go? Is Cowan going to be good as Falstaff?"

They began to talk shop, and soon the lights of Charnton could be seen ahead. The rain had stopped now, and the night was fine, though clouds still drifted across the pale face of the moon. Peter dropped Phyllis at the side door of the school, and then turned the car round to take Jennifer back to the lodge.

Alone together, as they had longed to be, constraint came upon them, and they could find nothing to say. Obscurely, Jennifer was anxious about Dick: if Peter had assessed Janine correctly she was not a good person to be with so young a man, although Phyllis was so completely unperturbed about it. Jennifer felt uneasy, and shivered as Peter stopped the car outside the lodge.

"Cold?" he asked, turning to look at her as he switched off the engine.

She shook her head and smiled.

"No, just a goose," she said. "Thank you for coming for us, Peter," she added. "Goodnight," and was out of the car in a moment.

He hovered behind her awkwardly, as she opened the door of the lodge; silhouetted against the darkening sky he looked tall and very thin, a lean black shape with faintly wavy hair.

"Goodnight," she said again, and disappeared.

The door closed quietly behind her, and Peter stood looking at it ruefully for a moment. Then he turned back and got into his car again. He saw a light come on upstairs, at the side of the building, as Jennifer reached her room; it dimmed as she drew the curtains.

Peter put his hands on the steering

wheel. "Oh dear," he said, aloud, "oh dear."

Nobody heard Dick when he drove up the drive, very much later; and Phyllis had been asleep for hours when he walked on airy stockinged feet past her door and into his own bedroom.

8

CHRISTOPHER was to sing a solo in the school concert. Miss Wayne had decreed it, four days after his mother had come down to the school and gone away again without speaking to him. When the singing lesson at which this pronouncement was made ended, he lingered behind after the other boys had gone, trying to nerve himself to consult Jennifer.

"Did you want to ask me something, Wilson?" she asked, as he hovered by the piano. His face was white and pinched again, and all his new vivacity had vanished.

"Miss Wayne, do you think my mother will come to the concert to hear me sing?" he asked at last, desperately.

"I'm sure she will, Wilson," said Jennifer; then, reflecting, wondered. "At least, if she isn't acting herself that day," she amended.

"She is awfully busy, you see, most of

the time," said Christopher. "She has to work very hard, or she would come and see me often." It seemed as if, by repeating his defence of his mother, Christopher hoped to convince himself.

"I expect so," said Jennifer.

"I'll do my very best at the concert, Miss Wayne," Christopher assured her earnestly.

"I know you will, Wilson," said Jennifer. "Now, hadn't you better run along? You'll be late for your next lesson."

He hurried off. Jennifer watched him go, and then, after a minute, philosophically switched her mind away from his problems to those of Jones I who was to play a Chopin nocturne at the concert, and did not know it yet.

Common Entrance had come and gone, with its attendant fears, and now the activities of the school were gearing round to the play. End of term exams did not loom on the horizon till this was over, and there were few people who were not concerned in one way or another with the approaching production. Boys could be heard loudly declaiming as they walked down the passages, and Phyllis had taken stock of the acting cupboard to see what must be revived and remodelled. She was always wardrobe mistress, and annually enlisted the matrons into her team of stitchers and tailors. Theirs was a pleasant life in the summer, for there was seldom much illness that term; and the boys wore so few clothes that mending was reduced to a minimum. While matron knitted for her many nieces and nephews, her younger assistants spent hours in the sea when the weather was good, or played tennis on the hard court at the end of the garden; between times Phyllis sternly made them stitch braid on to velvet doublets while they sunbathed, or take up hems on wide-skirted dresses.

Ronald was by this time wholeheartedly helping Peter, and was even forgetting to write his novel as he thought of new ways for Falstaff to win laughs. He was less self-conscious now; the boys respected him and obeyed him with little trouble. Dick Butler found this very irritating, for he could not quell them almost with a look in the way that Ronald could, and often had to shout to obtain order.

Jennifer had enjoyed the evening she

spent with Ronald at the concert; they were both happy listening to the music, and afterwards had an absorbing discussion about what they had heard. After that a real friendship grew between them in the most natural way, and with no more amorous undertones from Ronald. He decided that love was not for him at the moment, and found instead real satisfaction in getting to know the boys and in seeing their small successes.

Wilfrid Fitzgibbon took time off from among the tomatoes to run a recorder group. He said himself that his incipient deafness made it his duty to be the one to undertake this task, for the sounds produced were an insult to more sensitive ears. His musicians could be heard assiduously practising "The Bluebells of Scotland" and "The Skye Boat Song" which were to be their offerings at the concert.

Marion looked out the lists for the caterers, and the gardener tried to delay the blooming of the roses for fear there would be none on Parents' Day.

Phyllis spent a day writing out and addressing invitations, though it was well known that at least a quarter of the parents would forget to reply, so that the numbers must be guessed in any case. "Please say how many there will be in your party," she wrote on the back of the cards for the sixteenth year; and wondered, as she did each time, if there were not a more elegant and grammatical way of making this request.

On the Sunday evening after Phyllis and Jennifer had been to the theatre several members of the staff received sharp shocks. It was almost time for evening chapel: those boys who had been out with their parents had returned, and the last visiting car had driven away from the school. The boys were washing, before lining up to walk across the garden to the little private church which was in a corner of the grounds. Dick was the first to be startled: he was returning up the drive from the pub in the village where he had been to buy some cigarettes when a large chauffeur-driven car sped past him, going towards the school, and Janine's blonde head, under a wide-brimmed hat, poked out of the window. She beckoned him to join her, and he willingly climbed into the hired car beside her.

160

Geoffrey was the second person to be shocked when, glancing from his study window before going over to the chapel, he beheld his most lowly master stepping out of a large limousine and turning to hand down the blonde houri, as Geoffrey now thought of Mrs. Wilson.

Marion was the third to be surprised, when Geoffrey hastily summoned her and said that the actress had come to attend the service.

"She isn't fit to be admitted," he added.

"Perhaps it will do her good," suggested Marion optimistically. "Hell, she would come when I'm only wearing this old rag," she added, looking down disgustedly at her crisp green poplin dress.

"It looks a very nice rag to me, and you needn't worry about competition," said Geoffrey.

She made a face, then gave her belt a hitch and went into the hall, where she gathered up Janine and led her through the garden to the chapel.

Jennifer, sitting at the organ, was the next to be amazed: she heard a rustle among the boys as they turned their heads inquisitively to inspect the visitor, and a wave of Chanel 5 was wafted towards her by Janine's progress down the aisle.

Christopher, still lost in his misery though the reason for it had faded from the front of his mind, never noticed that anything unusual was happening. Parents often came to the morning service, but rarely stayed on in the evening; Geoffrey did not encourage them to spin out their farewells. An idea came to Jennifer as she looked at the little boy in his seat among the choir; he was staring vacantly into space while beside him Jones II sat picking his nose in a bored way. Jennifer was playing a voluntary, but she stopped at the end of a phrase and went over to Peter where he sat, a baritone, at the back of the choir. She whispered to him: he gave a startled glance in the direction of the congregation to where, sure enough, Janine sat beside Marion, then nodded. Jennifer crossed the chancel and bent to speak to Christopher. His face went pink, and he stared up at her before he too looked along the rows of pews and saw his mother. He gave Jennifer a wide smile and nodded vigorously in his turn. Jennifer spoke softly to the rest of the choir, then went back to her seat at the organ and began again to play.

Thus it was that Christopher sang by himself a large section of the aria that the choir had been industriously practising for that evening. Effortlessly, his pure young voice soared into the rafters of the building; there was no hesitation, and no struggle for pitch. It was a beautiful, almost perfect performance; and Jennifer thought his mother must have a heart of stone if she were not moved by it.

Everyone was determined to see that Janine should not escape again without speaking to her son. Phyllis collected him up as the choir filed out, and took him with her towards the main door of the chapel where Janine was holding court among a group of mainly reluctant attendants. On the fringe of them hovered Dick, looking flushed and rather scared, but holding his ground. Phyllis bored her way towards Janine, propelling Christopher before her.

"Here is Christopher, Mrs. Wilson," she said loudly, and added, in case Janine had not noticed his singing, "You sang very well, tonight, Wilson."

163

"Yes, well done," said Peter, smiling at Christopher.

"It was lovely, Wilson," said Marion.

"Good show, Wilson." Even Dick felt bound to speak, and knew he must probably also revise his attitude towards Christopher.

In the midst of all this Janine could scarcely be the only one not to add her praises.

"Why, Christopher," she cooed, and lightly touched his cheek with hers, carefully, lest her make-up smudge. "I never knew you could sing."

Christopher was spiritually transported to the top of Mount Everest. He could not speak, and did not need to; he stood and stared at his mother's pink and white face, and his eyes were enormous. Janine was now intent on being the perfect mother: a line from a play she had once been in came back to her, and she uttered it.

"My, what a big little boy you're getting," she exclaimed.

Marion laid her hand lightly on Christopher's dark head. "Christopher is singing a solo in the concert on Parents' Day next month," she said smoothly. "I hope you will come and hear him, Mrs. Wilson."

"But of course! How could I possibly stay away?" said Janine. She bent her face. Geoffrey, with rare malice, said afterwards that she was incapable of a real smile, for fear of causing a wrinkle.

"Do you promise, Mummy? You will come?" Christopher spoke at last.

"Of course, Christopher, of course," she said, and turned away from him, forgetting him already as she cast an extremely penetrating glance round the little semicircle of men grouped about her. Peter and Geoffrey stood in respectfully attentive attitudes, each with his hands clasped behind his back. Dick, proud with his secret knowledge, bravely remained in the company of his superiors. Janine scarcely noticed that Phyllis and Marion were present. She smiled at Dick: his extreme youth made up to her in its freshness for its own limitations and flattered her vanity, but it was Peter to whom she spoke; she was well aware that she had failed to subjugate him, and it was to remedy this that she had come to Arrowhurst this evening.

"Mr. Farquhar, have you been doing any more swimming lately?" she asked. "I so long to see where you do all this—there wasn't time when I came before. Won't you show me now?" And she put her hand lightly on Peter's arm and bore him away. He gave one horrified glance at the other two women, and then, realising that no one would rescue him and there was nothing else for it, fell into step beside her.

Dick watched them go. Rage filled him: unreasonably, he thought how dare Peter take her off like that? Peter was always interfering when he was not wanted. For a moment he thought of joining them, until the sudden realisation of his own youth and inexperience overwhelmed him. He clenched his fists; then he turned and slouched off.

"Come along, Wilson, time for cocoa," said Phyllis in her calm voice. "There, it was lovely that your mother came and heard you sing, wasn't it?" She walked him off towards the school, into which the other boys had vanished some minutes before, and he hopped and skipped along beside her.

"She's coming to the concert," he said,

"she promised. You heard, didn't you, Miss Norton?"

"I heard," said Phyllis. "Yes, I heard."

After this there was no holding Christopher. He forged ahead: he began to wield a useful bat: he swam a dozen strokes: and he sang like an angel. Amid her efforts to win competence from the other concert performers, Jennifer was profoundly relieved to know that he at least was note and word perfect beyond dispute. During these days she saw little of Peter outside school: his evenings were spent either bowling at the nets if it was fine, or more often rehearsing, or else unravelling lighting problems with Ronald, who had surprisingly revealed himself as a knowledgeable electrician and caused them to embark upon a new scheme of elaborate lighting in the gym. She herself was increasingly occupied with singing practice or the percussion band, and had been enlisted into the recorder group because Wilfrid said he must have at least one member of it who could keep time. They rehearsed in the spinney on Tuesdays and Thursdays, and Geoffrey said their melody was as the wailing of dispossessed ghosts when it came to the ear of the passer-by.

There were cricket matches twice a week, on Wednesdays and Saturdays, although one or two had to be scrapped because of wet weather. The passing of time now, though, was described always in relation to Parents' Day, and no one was able to look beyond this landmark on the calendar.

Geoffrey had years ago given up providing an outdoor summer entertainment for the parents. Fathers' cricket matches, with the senior players bursting out of ancient flannels, and struggling not to disgrace themselves as they panted up the pitch or fiercely brandished a boy's size bat, were, he thought, an overrated pastime. There were always at least forty offended fathers among those who had not been asked to play; only a few were thankful to be spared; and the ones he felt obliged to ask, though gratified, were, when it came to the actual day, reluctant. For two successive years a half gale had blown on the date, and Geoffrey had at last bowed to the unreliability of the climate and embarked instead upon dramatic productions. In the first years these were produced with plans A and B, for fine or wet weather; which operation must be decided at the latest half an hour before the performance was due to begin, and the weather had before now extinguished the most devoted parents' enthusiasm as they sat watching the frolicking Midsummer Night's dreamers through a curtain of misty rain. The disorder of herding two hundred cold and irritable parents into the gym half-way through the performance, and the mental strain of trying to decide whether or not to risk the whims of an angry sky, had at last proved to Geoffrey that it was wiser to expect bad weather and cater accordingly. So now the concert was always in the gym, and if it was a fine hot day Marion went about murmuring "It's so warm, we thought it would be more restful in the cool indoors," and all the parents thought happily how wise the Frosts were. After the concert there was a lavish stand-up tea in the dining-room, and then, if it was fine, the parents strolled round the grounds with their offspring, and inspected the handwork, carpentry, and lurid paintings that were on display, exhibiting, if not the talent of the boys, at least the ingenuity of their mentors. Later Geoffrey and Marion drank sherry with a chosen few of their favourite mothers and fathers in the drawing-room, and the evening usually ended with several of the boys who had acted as waiters at tea being sick as a result of loading themselves with more food than they could absorb.

This year the preparations were carried out as before. The appointed day came at last, and the impatient boys sat restively through the morning's lessons whilst the outside staff and some of the Sixth form moved the tables round in the dining hall and placed the chairs in the gym. Christopher woke early that morning, and lay in bed listening to the chirruping birds while his heart beat fast in anticipation. The day had come: today he would sing in front of the whole school, and be applauded, and his mother would be proud of him. He felt no nervousness, only excitement: his singing came as naturally to him as his breathing.

The visiting violin teacher arrived before lunch, wearing her best violet silk dress and an anxious expression. Some of the solo performers were pale with nerves, and Jennifer who was as unsure as Jones I himself about his Chopin nocturne, saw with dismay that he turned green and left the dining-room, unable to eat.

"It's cruel—why do we make them do it?" she said to Phyllis later as they pinned Falstaff into his doublet.

"Does them good. It's character-forming, and produces fortitude," said Phyllis. She gave a pat to the padded body of the actor and said, "There, now your mother won't know you, Cowan. Go along and wait with the others, and keep still or you'll come unstuffed." Falstaff waddled off, feeling very hot in his disguise, to join his friends who were sitting on benches in the boys' changing-room, hidden out of sight of their arriving parents.

"What a lovely girl Bradley makes," said Jennifer, as Phyllis picked up the skirt and bodice cut from an old dress of Marion's that the boy who was to play Lady Percy would wear.

"He feels an awful ass dressed as one," said Phyllis. "Peter miscast him, I think. He strides about so athletically. I must go

171

and get him ready. I told him not to come up here, he's hopeless at managing his skirts, so the fewer yards he has to walk the safer he'll be from rips." She picked up her box of pins and ready-threaded needles, and prepared to leave. "I expect you're nervous, Jenny, even if the boys aren't. It's the first time for you. Don't worry; it'll all be the same next year, and for a hundred years, and you'll probably be the only one who'll notice the wrong notes."

Jennifer laughed. "I expect you're right," she said. "I'd better go and make sure no one's lost his music. I wish we were in the first half, then we could relax and enjoy the play afterwards."

"Enjoy it, enjoy it," said Phyllis. "Worry won't make Jones I become inspired."

"I wish I hadn't picked him now," said Jennifer. "He doesn't really know the piece."

"He's a lazy young limb," said Phyllis, "but I expect he'll manage all right, he's been practising hard for the last half hour. Those Jones boys are all so musical they've got crotchets coming out of their ears—I don't think any of them could give a bad performance."

"Don't you? Well, I do," said Jennifer grimly. "The silly boy, he'll get himself really in a muddle if he goes on practising now. I'd better stop him."

"You leave him, or he'll be sick again, and anything's better than that," warned Phyllis.

For the past half hour matron and her assistants had been busy supervising the transformation of the boys who were not in the play. They had tumbled out of their green aertex shirts after lunch, and discarded the so-called grey corduroy shorts, white with age in some cases and black with mire in others, which they daily wore casually resting on their hips in the waistless manner of all small boys; now they were arrayed in grey flannel suits with the red school tie discreetly appearing, their hair neatly parted and their stockings pulled up.

By now the first parents were arriving. It was a matter of some conjecture among them as to whether they should arrive at the exact hour written on the invitation, or ten minutes sooner to be sure of getting a good seat, or ten minutes later as if for a cocktail party. The early arrivals sat self-consciously dotted about the gym with their sons, feeling conspicuous until the chairs began to fill up when the main rush came at zero hour exactly. Mothers smiled proudly, mostly beneath the brims of smart straw hats; husbands, many bored already, eased the creases in their best suits and sighed for a missed afternoon's golf. The new boys' parents, not yet sure of the form and knowing no one, tried to look insignificant, and the younger mothers realised they need not have worn hats after all.

Peter's cast of Shakespearian actors trooped into the wings from their assembly point in the changing rooms, fiercely made up with moustaches and rouged faces, and with Phyllis buttoning, stitching and re-pinning those for whom at the last moment the demands of nerves and of nature proved too much. At last, as the curtains jerkily drew apart, a hush fell upon the audience, and King Henry, truly looking shaken with care, though not wan under his ruddy false complexion, took the stage. The boy's voice, hesitant at first, strengthened as he got into his speech, and Peter, holding his edited and remodelled copy of the play, ready to prompt, began to relax. Ronald, working his lights beside him, had time to give the thumbs-up sign. They were off.

Where the text had been ruthlessly cut to allow for a sweeping précis of the whole play to be performed, Peter spoke a few twentieth-century sentences, off-stage, to explain and carry the action forward for the benefit of the many members of the audience, not only among the boys, who were unfamiliar with the original. After the high, piping voices of the youthful actors his own sounded very deep. Jennifer, sitting at the piano, ready to play the few incidental chords required to enliven proceedings, dreamed pleasantly as she listened to him. She was startled when a boy sidled up to her and whispered, under cover of the applause at the end of a speech by Hotspur, "Miss Wayne, do you know where Wilson is? He isn't with the choir. Mr. Fitzgibbon sent me to ask you."

"No." Jennifer looked up quickly. "Perhaps he's sitting with his mother?"

she suggested. "Go and look." Hastily she played a few battle chords, and the boy disappeared. He came back a few minutes later shaking his head.

"Find Miss Norton and tell her," Jennifer whispered.

The boy made off again, and in the gloom she tried to peer among the audience for Janine, whose clothes she was sure would be conspicuous. There were no curtains to the high windows in the gym; odd bits of cloth had been draped to cut out the brightest light whilst still admitting the air, and the result was rather like the opacity of an aquarium. Jennifer could not see her among the navy and white or flowery mothers.

"' O Harry, thou hast robbed me of my youth,'" cried Hotspur from the stage. With gusto he went through his speech, and died with fine histrionic realism and gruesome moans while Prince Henry committed him to the worms. The curtain fell to tumultuous applause, and Peter thankfully mopped his brow.

"Jolly good, boys, it went splendidly," he said to his troupe. "Well done, Brown —Cowan—you were all first-class. Now hurry up and get changed." He chivvied them along to the changing-rooms where they were to disrobe during the interval, catching the back of Lady Percy's skirt as she went along, and hoisting it up behind.

"You'll fall over this, Bradley," he warned, "better hold it."

"I'll take it off," said "Lady Percy," and was to be seen a minute later running down the passage wearing a wimple on her head, a green velvet bodice, and skimpy white underpants.

Phyllis was surrounded in the changing-room by a dozen or so boys struggling out of their costumes, while matron lined up those already stripped and with cold cream and soap began to remove the make-up from their heated faces.

"Have you seen Wilson anywhere?" Phyllis asked Peter, across the head of a boy from whom she was removing his leather jerkin.

"No." Peter looked surprised. "Surely he's with the choir?" He began unbuttoning Bradley's bodice back. "Hurry up, you boys who are singing, there isn't much time."

"Il a disparu, sa mère n'est pas arrivée," muttered Phyllis.

Peter stared, holding the bodice half on and half off Bradley so that he looked as if his head was in a sack.

"You must be wrong!"

"No, je ne suis pas wrong," said Phyllis, whose French was limited. "J'ai cherché pour lui dans tout l'école, et matron aussi." She made a face, indicative of the pitcher-like quality of the ears of the boys about her. Peter automatically released Bradley from his Blind Man's Buff position and sent him off to matron to be cleaned, and at that moment, white-faced, Jennifer entered the room.

"Not here," said Phyllis quickly.

"I'll be right with you," said Peter to Jennifer. "Boys, those of you who are in the concert, get dressed as fast as you can. The rest of you help them and clear up in here. Then you can go and sit with your parents." He turned as he spoke, and hurried away after Jennifer.

"He hasn't been seen all afternoon," she told him outside. "He was waiting with the others in the hall when the parents were arriving, and no one's seen him since.

178

Dick saw him alone there, just before the play began, and told him to go to the gym, but he can't have done so."

"Didn't his mother come then?" asked Peter.

"Evidently not."

"The bitch," said Peter.

"What are we to do?" asked Jennifer. "Where can he have got to? Dick and some of the others are looking in the grounds now, and Phyllis and matron have searched the whole of the building."

"He must be hiding—he could be anywhere." Peter thought rapidly. "Does Geoff know, and Marion?"

"No," said Jennifer.

"Write a note to Marion and get a boy to give it to her," Peter said. "I'll collect as many of the staff as I can and we'll go right through the place. He could be in a cupboard somewhere. We mustn't let the parents know something's wrong."

"I'll change the programme round and put his song at the end," said Jennifer. "Maybe he'll have turned up by then. He can't have got stage fright—he was longing for today."

"He could be watching for his mother

somewhere. If she comes he'll probably appear. You carry on, Jenny. I expect he'll turn up."

"All right." She went away, and he hurried into the gym to enlist some members of the staff for the search. Jennifer scribbled a note and beckoned a sensible boy to her side. He slid off and delivered it to Marion. Jennifer saw her eyebrows fly up as she read it; she folded it neatly, and with a murmured remark to the head boy's father, beside whom she sat, leaned across and handed it to Geoffrey. Jennifer took her seat at the piano; the choir, minus Christopher, filed on to the stage, and it was time to begin.

There was no sign of Christopher when the appointed moment for his solo was reached, so Jones I, pale and trembling, was launched uncertainly before time upon his Chopin nocturne.

Meanwhile Peter organised a methodical search all through the school. With Dick, Ronald and some others he went again over the whole building, looking in cupboards and on top of them, under beds, behind curtains, and searching even Geoffrey's and Marion's private rooms. At intervals one of them went back to the gym in case in the meantime Christopher had reappeared, and then, when he still had not been found, they moved out to search the grounds. The sky, which earlier had been clear, was leaden now, and in the distance thunder rumbled. The concert must be nearly over, Peter thought. Poor Jenny, he knew she was nervous, and wondered how it was going. He pushed his way through the bushes in the spinney, calling Christopher by name, but there was no sight or sign of the boy.

Back in the gym, Jennifer announced that owing to the indisposition of Wilson the solo chorale would be sung by Jones II, and that young man, stunned by the unexpected limelight, gave a very creditable performance, to the dewy-eyed delight of his fond mother.

At last, with a scraping of chairs, the concert ended. The audience, stiff from a long sojourn on hard seats, rose thankfully, and trooped in to tea.

Phyllis waylaid Geoffrey in the passage.

"Not turned up yet," she said.

"Try the beach," said Geoffrey.

"The police?" asked Phyllis.

"Not yet," said Geoffrey. He went on into the dining-room, and was at once absorbed into the crowd of parents who wanted to hear his views on the sporting, academic and moral progress of their sons, and to sing the praises of their performances. Little boys, loaded with plates of bridge rolls spread with exotic arrangements of tomato, cucumber and sardines, or bearing cream cakes and sugar buns, circled about waist-high amid the crowd, stuffing food into their own mouths meanwhile in a single-minded way like conveyor belts working overtime. Marion, who was wearing a tight-fitting coffee-coloured silk dress and who was as always more elegant than any other woman present, floated about watching for lost-looking parents to introduce to others, and finding agreeable things to say to everyone about their sons. She never hesitated for more than a moment over names, even among the new parents, though she had only met some of them once before. It was Geoffrey who, on a famous occasion, had delivered to some startled parents, waiting in the hall one Sunday for their son, quite the wrong Michael of the many in the school. When she first came to Arrowhurst, Marion had soon realised that in a community where the boys were addressed only by their surnames she, if no one else, must also know their others. It was a task, that first term, to get them pat, complicated by the Robins and Tims who had not all been christened so, and by the boys with three or four Christian names who were called by any of them except the first; but she mastered it, and now it was a simple matter to learn the new ones every term. She and Phyllis often used them when they talked to the boys; Geoffrey teased them about it and called it their softening feminine touch.

Though she never looked forward with any eagerness to Parents' Day, Marion always found in the end that she enjoyed it. Most of the parents were very pleasant, though a few were notorious for their boring conversation or patronising manner, but Marion was easily a match for these. In the main the fathers and mothers had an attitude of hesitant affability; they were so anxious not to shame their sons by saying the wrong things that by their humilty an outsider would have supposed them to be under an overwhelming obligation to the headmaster and his staff, instead of being at the signing end of the cheques. Most of the parents did in fact feel that no monetary recompense was adequate for the way in which under Geoffrey's guidance their boys were helped to develop character and self-reliance, and no boy at Arrowhurst had, in present memory, failed his Common Entrance. Those who thought about such things realised that Marion and Geoffrey made almost no profit from their school: they cleared their living expenses, and anything that was to spare was used in maintaining the building or acquiring new and improved equipment for the boys; at present, because of the increasing amount of oil in the sea, plans were on foot for a swimming pool; and Geoffrey always struggled to keep the fees from rising, for many parents denied themselves the luxuries of life to meet them.

Presently the last car had reluctantly driven away down the drive, and the boys were having their high tea. Geoffrey and Marion went out of the drawing-room over the lawn to meet the searchers wearily trooping back from their vain efforts to find Christopher on the beach.

They returned to the house in silence.

"Should we ask any of his friends if they know where he is, sir?" suggested Ronald.

"We don't want a panic." Geoffrey was thinking aloud; his face was haggard, and he suddenly looked quite old to the young man who stood before him.

"A few of the older boys know he's missing," said Peter. "They realised, when he didn't turn up to sing, but I told them to keep quiet about it."

"I see." Geoffrey nodded thoughtfully. "Who is his particular friend, Peter?"

"I should say Jones II," said Peter. "I know they go bug-hunting together."

"Better get him down here then," said Geoffrey. "Don't scare him. Who's on duty upstairs?"

"I think everyone's helping tonight; the boys are tired," said Peter. "I know Phyllis is there, she was with us but she came back about ten minutes before we did."

"See her, then," said Geoffrey. "Get her to cope. If this produces nothing we'll have to call the police." He sat down wearily while Peter hurried out.

"It'll be all right, Geoff. He's probably in Charnton," said Marion, with a confidence she was far from feeling. She put a hand on his shoulder for a moment, and looked round the room at the anxious faces of the men who had been combing the grounds for so long. "Nothing can have happened to him," she declared firmly.

In a few minutes Phyllis entered the room, followed by an awed Jones II who had not been into this august apartment since he had come to tea with Marion on his first Sunday as a new boy. He was dressed in a very short, threadbare, brown dressing-gown; below it, faded striped pyjama legs ended well above his bony ankles. Phyllis pushed him forward over the threshold, and he stood, very small and unusually timid, staring at the group of silent adults who seemed to fill the room.

"Jones, ah—you sang very well today. Good boy," Geoffrey began.

"Thank you, sir," said Jones primly.

"Now Jones," Geoffrey hesitated. "Where—er, when did you last see

Wilson?" He thought it was best to plunge, and not alarm the boy with preparatory remarks.

Jones frowned, concentrating deeply. "He was in the hall," he volunteered at last.

"When was this?" asked Geoffrey, his voice sharp with fatigue and nervousness. The little boy looked startled, and Phyllis glowered at Geoffrey, whose next remark was gentler.

"Try to remember," he urged.

"Before the concert," said Jones.

"When you were waiting for your parents to arrive?"

"Yes, sir. He was waiting for his mater too," said Jones more confidently.

"You haven't seen him since then? You're quite sure?"

Jones pondered solemnly for a moment. "I'm quite sure," he said at last.

"I see," said Geoffrey. They were no further forward.

Jones, made bold by the unusual circumstances, said then, "Oh sir, where is he? Is he lost? Has he run away?"

"We don't know where he is, Jones, but I'm sure he hasn't run away, that would be very foolish," said Geoffrey firmly. "He must be hiding somewhere. He may have been afraid of singing."

"Oh no, sir, he wasn't," said Jones at once, almost with derision. "He liked it, he didn't mind a bit. He was looking forward to it, he wanted his mater to see him. Non-swank, of course," he added hastily, fearing to betray his friend.

"You can't think of any special place where he might go to hide?" asked Geoffrey.

"No sir—unless the pavilion? That would be a good place, or in a games locker?" Jones tried to be helpful.

"We'll try them," Geoffrey promised, knowing very well that they had already been searched.

"Oh sir, please find him." Jones' voice quavered suddenly as his Welsh imagination conveyed to him a fraction of the true position. His lip trembled.

"We'll find him, Jones, don't worry. He'll come in when it begins to get dark," said Geoffrey, wishing he was as sure of this as he hoped he sounded.

"Come along, David. Back to bed," said Phyllis. "Now don't you worry, you've been a great help, and we'll soon find him. We'll put him in the sickroom, though, tonight, so don't be surprised if he isn't in the dormitory when you wake up tomorrow." Talking cheerfully, she led him back upstairs.

Geoffrey looked at Peter. "How far along the shore did you go?" he asked.

"We went right up to the point. He couldn't have got past it, the tide's right up, and you know it's only ever clear for a very short time at low water. We've been right along the top of the cliff nearly as far as Charnton, and to Fadgeley the other way. You'll have to get the police, Geoffrey. It'll be dark soon, and it's very stormy." Peter's mouth was set: he would have called the police two hours before had Geoffrey been away and he in charge.

The headmaster put out his hand and lifted the telephone from its hook.

"Go and get something to eat," he said, as he dialled the number. "We'll have to go out again."

"And his mother? You'll have to tell her," said Peter, insistently.

Geoffrey looked up. His face was lined and weary. Peter felt a fleeting pity for

189

him, but it was swept away by the urgency of the present situation with which Geoffrey seemed suddenly unable to cope. "I'll ring her," he said.

9

SHE'S late, Christopher thought at first, when his mother did not come. He stood in the hall, stiffly, so that his socks would stay up and his hair remain parted, and kept his eyes fixed on the door through which she would arrive. Gradually the number of waiting boys dwindled, till only three others were left. Presently they, too, had gone, and he was alone. Mr. Butler passed quickly through and told him to go down to the gym, but he stayed in the corner by the window, a motionless sentinel, and two other masters hurrying by never noticed him.

"She'll come in a minute," Christopher thought, blinking hard. His throat felt peculiar, and he was afraid he might blub. He knew that mother's play had not opened yet in London, so there couldn't be a matinée, but probably she was rehearsing late. He went to the open front door and looked out. Everything was quiet. Rows of cars stood neatly parked down the drive and on the field, mostly small saloons and brakes, but there was one large Rolls and there were several Bentleys. The clock struck three: the play would have begun. Christopher walked slowly down the passage to the gym, shuffling his feet. From within could be heard the voice of Hotspur, loudly declaiming.

Perhaps she's just arriving now, and there's no one to show her the way, Christopher thought, in sudden panic. He ran back to the hall, but it was just as he had left it, still and deserted. The polished floor echoed his lonely footsteps, and the clock ticked on. Christopher went slowly out, down the front steps and on to the drive. She's on her way, he thought, she promised: and he began to walk down the drive, pausing to listen when he thought he heard the sound of a car, but no one came.

"I'll go to meet her," he decided in a formless way, and went on walking. Presently he forgot where he was going, and why, because he was crying.

"She said she'd come, she said, she said," he mourned aloud, plodding on down the narrow road that ran past the school to Charnton. It was not till he reached the outskirts of the town that he remembered London lay the other way, and that he would never meet his mother here. Suddenly he realised, with terror, what he had done. He had walked into Charnton from school, and he was supposed to be sitting in the gym waiting to sing.

"I promised Mr. Farquhar I wouldn't go out of school again," he recalled, in horror. He was afraid. What should he do? Perhaps he could get back to school without being found out. What was the time? Summoning his courage, he asked a passing woman and learned that it was half-past four. The concert would be nearly over. He looked about him dazedly, made stupid by grief and fright, and saw that he was near the station where he had arrived at the beginning of term.

"Perhaps she's ill, I'd better go home and see," he thought wildly, and before his resolution failed he went to ask for a ticket, but drew back from the glass window as he remembered that he had no money. There was a telephone box in the booking hall, so he went into it and pressed button B. It gave out a metallic groan, and that was all.

Christopher went out into the road again. A policeman who had seen him enter the station eyed him for a moment, and then walked over to him.

"You all right, sonny? Not lost?" he asked.

"No, oh no, thank you," said Christopher hastily. He hitched his trousers up nervously, and went off down the road towards the shore. No plan had formed in his head, but he began to walk along the beach towards Arrowhurst. The sky was heavy now, and a few spots of rain fell. Thunder rumbled in the distance, and he shivered. He hurried along, while lightning streaked the sky and the ominous noise grew louder. The waves crashed and fell back on his right, thudding against the boulders that strewed the beach, and sending showers of spray into the air as they broke. There were shingle patches over which he stumbled, scrunching, until he reached the jutting mass of cliff round which lay the two clear miles of sand that ended below the school. Already the incoming tide, nearly full, was lapping round the foot of the promontory; Christopher could not get round. He suddenly felt very tired. Behind him, Charnton's houses seemed miles away; he could not go back. He looked up at the cliff face; if he could climb above the reach of the water he might be able to work his way around the point until he could get down again on to the beach.

He began to clamber up the chalky cliff, hampered by the tight, outgrown jacket of his flannel suit. Up and up he went, seeking hand and foot holds in the rock, and trying all the time to work his way sideways round the point. Once he looked down and saw the water, far below, boiling as it surged against the outcrop and was sucked back again by the tide. Even as he climbed it had risen higher: somehow he managed to crawl and creep round the point at last, and when he had done so Christopher saw that there were only a few feet of sand left between the water's edge and the bottom of the cliff for as far as he could see. He could not go down, but must manage to work his way along the cliff face still further, or else climb to the top. Terrified, he pulled himself up a few more feet. The wind was howling now, and the noise of the sea grew loud. He wondered what the time was, and thought with longing of the safety of school. He was hungry, too. On he went: several times his foot slipped and sent a shower of chalky stones crashing down into the steadily mounting waves below. Once a tussock of grass came away in his hand as he grasped it, and he paused, shaking, crouching against the cliff, until he was able to reach out and feel for another hand-hold. Now his mind became empty of everything except the necessity for continuing ever upward. He was concerned only with the primitive struggle for survival. He was a few feet from the top of the cliff when a rock fell away from under him, and he went tumbling down. Only some gulls, wheeling above him in the wind, heard his screams before they swooped away, shrieking, to seek the shelter of the inland fields.

Then there was silence.

10

THE police were efficient. By half-past nine that night they had established that a boy answering to Christopher's description had been seen in Charnton.

"He may still be in the district, or he may have got a bus, or thumbed a lift somewhere," said Colonel Maude, the Chief Constable, who was a personal friend of Geoffrey's, and who now sat in the drawing-room at Arrowhurst conducting operations. "We're making enquiries, but meanwhile we mustn't rule out the possibility that the boy seen at the station was a different boy; or that, if it was him, young Wilson has returned to school and is hiding somewhere about the premises. Now, where have you searched?"

Geoffrey described the detailed hunt made by his staff.

"Hm. Supposing he had come back, he could be hiding now in one of the places where you've looked, scared of facing retribution," said Colonel Maude, stroking his clipped white moustache thoughtfully. "That means we must make another thorough search of the grounds and buildings. Wherever he is, he'll be tired by this time—he could be sleeping in a haystack, y'know. Kids have done that before and not been found for days."

Geoffrey blanched at the prospect of Christopher being absent, whereabouts unknown, for several days.

The Chief Constable rose to his feet.

"Well, now. We'll get teams of searchers organised. We'll need all your staff, Frost, and I'll put as many men on it as I can spare. If he doesn't turn up by the time it gets dark we'll call in the army tomorrow. I'm afraid it's no use trying to get a helicopter up tonight—the weather is far too bad, but it may be better in the morning." He turned to the inspector who stood beside him and they held a brief, brisk discussion. Then the inspector went away to organise the search.

In the hall he found Peter and most of the staff, in mackintoshes and wellingtons, with torches in their hands, silently waiting. All the masters were there, even

Wilfrid, the oldest; and the gardeners and the odd-job man; and all the female staff except for Phyllis and Matron.

The inspector gave them their instructions, and they joined the policemen already mustered. It was agreed that while they looked outside, Phyllis, Matron and the three resident maids should comb the inside of the building yet again; most of the domestic staff came daily from Charnton and had now gone home, unaware of the situation at the school.

So the long night began. Marion, wearing slacks and an oilskin, came into the drawing-room as the parties of searchers were spreading out over the grounds outside.

"I'm going, too, Geoffrey," she said. "It will soon be dark—we need everybody."

"I'm coming too," said Geoffrey, getting up.

Marion pushed him down again.

"No, you're not," she ordered. "You're very tired, and if you come you'll only make yourself ill. Besides, someone must be here, in case Mrs. Wilson telephones. In any case I think you should keep on ringing her every quarter of an hour. She must be told as soon as we can get hold of her, and you can't expect Phyllis to hold that baby for you."

"I suppose you're right," said Geoffrey. He felt utterly exhausted; strain and tribulation always exposed his weakness.

"Don't worry too much, Geoff," said Marion more gently. "We'll find him," she added, and was gone.

Geoffrey sat alone in the darkening room. Every so often he dialled the exchange and rang Janine's London number, but there was never a reply. From the garden came the sound of men's voices, calling; but presently the noises ceased as the search moved away, and he sat on in silence. His mind was full of the child who was missing, and his conscience was heavy. He had not given enough thought to this little boy; both Phyllis and Peter had been anxious about him; but he, who was ultimately responsible, had been content to let them do the worrying without himself trying to discover the cause of Christopher's difficulties. Lately the boy's work had been better, and he had shown such a pronounced all-round improvement that Geoffrey had been satisfied: now he knew that something must have been wrong which he might have noticed if he had given it more thought. Such a catastrophe had not happened at Arrowhurst in all the years that Geoffrey had been a master; the one other boy who had run away had been found almost before he was missed. Now Geoffrey was mortified to think that the prospect of harmful publicity for the school should even occur to him when Christopher's life might be in danger. Despair and self-disgust settled upon him.

Presently the door opened and Phyllis entered.

"All in the dark, Geoff?" she said, her voice calm as ever, as though it was a normal evening.

"Hullo, Phyl." Geoffrey roused himself a little. "No luck, I suppose?"

"No." She switched on the light, and went to draw the curtains across the windows. "What a night," she said, pausing with her hand on the curtain to listen to the howling of the wind. "They'll all be soaked through. No, he isn't in the house."

"You didn't go with the search parties?" he stated.

"Do you think I should have? You wanted to, I suppose," she said, bending down to turn on the electric fire. "Matron and I decided we were more use here. Someone will have to see to hot drinks for the searchers, and hot bottles and things for when the child is found. Besides, we've ninety-nine other boys to think about, four already in the sick-room with colds, and three who are bilious after stuffing themselves this afternoon."

"What a practical person you are, Phyl," said Geoffrey. "You're right, of course."

"It's always easier to be out doing things than sitting still waiting for them to happen," said Phyllis. "But the sitting part is often just as necessary." She turned to look at Geoffrey, and the sight of him sitting hunched in his chair, his face grey, made her heart contract.

"Brr, it's cold," she said. "Come nearer to the fire, Geoffrey, you look perished."

Obediently he drew his chair forward, closer to the bright metallic glow.

"Do you think they'll find him?" he asked.

"Of course they will," said Phyllis emphatically. "The entire police force in the county is out looking for him."

"It's such a dreadful night," said Geoffrey. "He may have had an accident."

"He's probably sitting by the fire in some comfortable farmhouse, if we did but know it, being fêted," said Phyllis. "Young limb."

"Phyl, what have I done? How could this happen?" asked Geoffrey, rubbing the ache in his forehead with the back of his hand.

"The child's mother didn't turn up. He was counting on singing in front of her," said Phyllis. "It's as simple as that. It's her fault, not yours. If she wasn't able to come she should have sent a message—but not to turn up—well, some boys might not mind, but with a sensitive little chap like Christopher it's quite understandable that he should rush off and hide."

"But he did sing in front of her, in chapel that time," said Geoffrey.

"Yes, I know he did, but this would

have been more glorious, and he was building on it. He was always saying his mother would be pleased when he could swim, or if he had a high place in form, and so on. Peter and the others were talking about it in the hall tonight, before they went out. He seemed obsessed by the desire to impress her with some achievement."

"I see you talk about him in the past tense, too, Phyl," said Geoffrey bitterly.

"Oh, Geoff, I'm sure he'll be all right," said Phyllis. "For goodness' sake take a grip on yourself. Don't expect the worst till it's happened." She got up and went to a cupboard in the corner of the room. "You need a drink," she said, "and so do I. Here." She took out some glasses and poured out two large whiskies, splashed some soda-water into them, and gave him one.

"Thanks, Phyl," said Geoffrey, taking a swallow of his. "Sorry," he added.

"Oh, that's all right," said Phyllis gruffly. "Sorry to blast at you."

"I deserved it," said Geoffrey. "If only I'd paid more attention to the boy! But I just thought he was homesick."

"So did we all. The penny's only really just dropped," said Phyllis generously.

Geoffrey, bent on self-abasement, said, "I rely too much on Peter. He's extraordinarily able, but he's too young to have the experience that I should have got after all these years."

"You're being very silly, Geoffrey," said Phyllis. "There has to be a first time for everything, and this is your first taste of this particular crisis. Let's hope it will be the last too. Don't drag Peter into it like that. He's splendid, and you know he is; he has a real gift for dealing with boys which is equal to years of experience. You're supposed to rely on him; you aren't strong, and he's your deputy. Isn't half the secret of having authority to know when to delegate it? We don't often get problems like Christopher Wilson, and I blame myself for not keeping an eye on him today. I knew how much he was counting on this, and I also wondered once or twice if Mrs. W. would turn up. I should have done more about it."

"It's no good going on trying to dole out the blame," said Geoffrey. The whisky was making him feel better. "This is one of our failures."

"It's something we can help to mend when he gets back," said Phyllis briskly. "Have you got on to his mother yet?"

"No, there's still no reply," said Geoffrey. "I'll have another try now."

He rang the exchange again, but the London number still did not answer.

"What about the grandmother? Do you think you should get in touch with her?" suggested Phyllis.

"I did consider it, but what good will it do? She's old and very frail, and she would be caused anxiety which may be quite unnecessary. If he isn't found by morning, and if I still haven't got hold of the mother, then I'll ring the old lady," he said.

Phyllis nodded. "Poor little boy. He must have been so unhappy," she said.

Geoffrey sat slowly rolling the dregs of whisky round in his glass. Then he said, "What a long time it is since we had a crisis, Phyl."

"Thank goodness," replied Phyllis promptly. "Freeman's appendix was the last, wasn't it?"

"Yes. That was a bad night," said Geoffrey, remembering.

"Poor Mrs. Freeman, sitting here crying throughout the time when he was having the operation, I'll never forget it," said Phyllis with feeling.

"Whisky seems to be your remedy for all crises," said Geoffrey. "I remember you made her rather drunk that night, pouring it into her."

"It was the only thing to do, poor soul," said Phyllis. "She forgot it all when she'd slept it off. Think how mortified she'd have been later to realise in the cold light of day how she'd sobbed all over you."

"They are odd, the parents," Geoffrey mused. "The most unlikely ones weep. I would never have expected her to give way. Do you remember when Peterson had pneumonia and really was ill? Mrs. Peterson was calmer than any of us."

"Yes, she was calm, but so were we, Geoff," said Phyllis with a smile. "Don't be unjust to us. Crises bring out the best in people, don't you find?"

"Not always. This one's brought out all the worst in me, but all the best in you," said Geoffrey. "Here have I been wallowing in self-abnegation, while you are as calm and dependable as the Rock of Gibraltar."

Phyllis only said, "I think you'd better have some more whisky, Geoffrey. The night's still very young."

Under the directions of the police the search parties were deployed around the school. Some went down to the rock-strewn shore, while others fanned out across the playing fields and then slowly moved on over the surrounding farmland. They found a cat with a new family of kittens lying in some hay in a barn, and they found a pair of lovers seeking privacy in a hut on the beach, but they did not find Christopher. When it was quite dark the police called off the search until first light, when they would set out again, and have the help of helicopters.

Marion, standing in the drive as the red tail lights of the police cars disappeared, said, "Peter, I don't know about you, but I can't go to bed leaving that child lost somewhere out here. I can't believe he's gone far, we'd have had news of him if that had happened. It may be quite useless, but we haven't been over the inland fields across the Charnton road. I want to try there."

"I don't think any of us could rest tonight," said Peter. "I'll come, of course."

One by one the others all said the same, and once more they set off, with torches and sticks, spread out in a wide cordon in the meadow land on the side of the road away from the sea. It was no longer raining, but their damp mackintoshes clung to them, and their hands and faces were torn and scratched as they struggled over brambles and hedges in the darkness. When they had gone some way without success they swung round, and, in a circling movement, made the return to Arrowhurst across another arc of unexplored land.

Jennifer was on the outside of the long line as they came slowly back through the dark night. She was so tired that she had almost lost sight of the reason for the search. She plodded on in her wellington boots, throwing the beam of her torch before her. She could see the winking lights of the other torches on her left, and hear shouts as Christopher's name was called. The lights of the school building grew nearer, and she realised that they were back, and had not found the child. Suddenly, on an impulse, when she reached the boundary of the playing fields, she turned away. Her longing for a hot bath and bed was the foremost thing in her mind, and she was ashamed of her frailty. I must try just once more, she thought, obscurely, and began to walk slowly back along the cliff towards Charnton.

The tide was going out now, and, as it turned, the wind had dropped a little; under the cliffs the sea heaved and sighed like a chorus of asthmatic ghosts. Jennifer walked along, her torch piercing the gloom with a thin finger of light. She stopped when she came to the point that jutted out into the sea before Charnton beach, and rested for a moment, staring out across the water: it looked like an angry monster boiling below, black and oily; the night was too dark for her to distinguish the whiteness of the spume. Suddenly she stiffened: above the wind and the crash of the waves she had heard another sound. She listened again. Yes, there it was, repeated, very faint, like the cry of a bird. It seemed to come from beneath her. She went closer to the cliff edge and crouched on the ground, listening intently; then, as her trained ear pin-pointed the direction whence the sound came, she began to move slowly back towards the school. Soon she could distinguish more than the faint noise that she had heard at first: "'Oh, soldier, soldier, won't you marry me, with your musket, fife and drum?'" The piping words were hurled up at her and borne away again by the eddying wind.

"'Oh, no, sweet maid, I cannot marry thee, for I have no shoes to put on,'" Jennifer heard quite plainly. A wild surge of relief and excitement came over her. Abruptly the singing ceased: she called at once, "Christopher, Christopher," but there was no reply. Then she lay down on her stomach on the wet grass and flashed her torch over the cliff edge, at the same time calling; but the wind that had blown Christopher's pathetic voice up to her threw her own words back into her throat. She could see nothing but inky blackness below. She remembered that she was alone, and tried to think calmly. It would take at least half an hour to reach anyone who could bring aid to Christopher; there were no houses between here and Arrowhurst, and Charnton was nearly as far. Once again she shone the torch, and suddenly heard a faint cry, "Help, he-elp!" She flashed her torch on and off several times; Christopher could not hear her voice, but he might thus understand that she had heard his. Then, leaning over as far as she dared, she shone the torch carefully over the rocks immediately below her. They looked almost sheer; it appeared impossible to climb down. Reason told her that she should go at once for help, men with ropes who would know the best way of getting Christopher up, but when she heard him start to scream she kicked off her clumsy boots and swung her legs over the cliff.

There were ledges and cracks. She shone the torch below her and looked for a fresh foothold; then, having reached it, she shone it again to find another; she climbed down, feeling the sharpness of the rocks with her stockinged feet as she went, and holding the torch in her mouth while she groped for handholds. The screaming went on and on, high-pitched and piercing, and then abruptly stopped: the silence was almost worse to hear than the terror in those screams. Then, suddenly, and much louder, she heard, "'Oh, soldier, soldier,'" begin again, in a queer, hoarse, tuneless voice. She pointed the torch down and shouted but Christopher did not listen. He could see the light flashing erratically about twenty feet above him, but he was beyond the power of thought and could not help to guide his rescuer to where he lay. Jennifer concentrated on moving towards the sound of the voice: then, suddenly, she saw him. He was lying in a heap on a little ledge just a few yards below her.

Christopher lay and watched the light draw closer, still droning on with his song, like a dirge, all on one note. He never doubted that she would reach him, and he was not really surprised to find it was Miss Wayne, but he fainted again as soon as she arrived.

Jennifer examined their predicament in the light of the torch. Christopher was soaked with rain: he lay with both legs doubled up under him, and blood from a cut on his head had congealed on his face. She could not attempt to get him up the cliff alone. Bitterly she chided herself for what she had so impetuously done; she ought to have left him alone and gone for proper help.

She laid the torch on the rock, where it sent a small comforting glow into the night. She held his cold, wet hands, and crouched beside him on the narrow ledge which was only just wide enough for them both.

"It's all right, Christopher," she said, when she saw his eyes open and blink uncomprehendingly. "You'll soon be safe. Don't worry." She patted his hands, and then managed to raise his head and shoulders a little. Somehow, hardly daring to move for fear she sent them both toppling downwards, Jennifer got her mackintosh off and removed the cardigan she wore underneath it. Slowly and carefully she stripped off Christopher's sodden grey jacket and put him into her jersey. She pulled his legs from their unnatural twisted position under his shivering body and wrapped him tightly in her raincoat;

more damage to them must be risked if the worse peril from exposure could be avoided. There was some chocolate in her pocket, and she broke a small piece off to give to him. He was quiet and unprotesting under her ministrations, and she realised that he had touched the ultimate in despair when he screamed before she came. She knew then that even if they perished together she had been right to climb down to him.

The jersey was warm from her body, and she put her arms round him and held him as best she could, keeping the worst of the wind away. She gave him some more chocolate, and then she said, "Now, Christopher, we'll just have to wait a little while for the others to come with ladders and things to get us up the cliff. I'll keep flashing my torch so that they can see where we are."

"They'll come soon, I s'pose," he said, quite sensibly.

"Yes, they won't be long," she answered. She began to switch the little beam of the torch on and off, shining it towards the school, until she realised that it was growing dim as the battery started to fail. Her heart sank.

Christopher stirred against her shoulder.

"Why have you stopped signalling?" he asked.

"We'll wait a little while, and then start again. We don't want to use up the battery," she said calmly. "We must leave some light in it so as to guide them to us. Let's do some singing."

She began to sing, and intermittently Christopher joined in. Jennifer ranged through all the cheerful songs she could remember, and then they started on hymns. Every few minutes she switched on the torch and signalled SOS, the only Morse she knew.

The rain had stopped; coldly the wind blew against the cliff, and the pair who huddled there. Jennifer dared not look downwards; shivering in her thin dress, she clung to the thought, "If he will stay alive till morning, we shall be found."

One by one the weary staff filed into the drawing-room, leaving a trail of damp footsteps across Marion's Persian carpet. They were all pale with exhaustion, dirty and bedraggled. Phyllis hurried away to fetch the hot Bovril she had prepared. It seemed, she thought, her lot in life to provide beverages in crises. When she returned with the heavy tray they were all sitting down in their stockinged feet; a row of gum boots stood by the door, and a pile of dripping raincoats had been dumped on the hall floor. No one was talking: cigarette smoke filled the room with a faint haze; and Phyliis handed round the mugs of Bovril silently. No one knew what to say, and even their murmured thanks seemed out of place.

Into this scene erupted Peter from the garden.

"Where's Jennifer?" he demanded.

"Isn't she here?" Phyllis looked round the assembled company: everyone stared wearily back at her, and then shifted their gaze to look at Peter, who stood in the french window with his hair on end and his eyes dark with fatigue and fear.

"But she was with you," said Phyllis slowly. "I thought you were all together."

"We were. At least, we were meant to be. Butler, she was next to you, didn't you see her torch?" Peter rounded on Dick, who sat smoking on the sofa.

"Yes, she was there all the time," he said sulkily, flicking ash on the floor. It was just like Peter to pick on him. His mind was extremely confused: he was very foolish, but he understood the gravity of Christopher's disappearance; however he resented the implication that Janine was responsible, and was infuriated that the boy had created a situation where she could be criticised.

"She's probably gone for some shoes, she'll be here in a minute," said Phyllis sensibly. "Here, have some Bovril, Peter, while it's hot."

But after ten long minutes Jennifer had not appeared.

"God, don't say she's lost now," said Geoffrey wearily.

Peter had turned very white, beneath the dirt and scratches on his face.

"We must find her," he said. "When did you last see her torch, Butler? Now think hard." He advanced into the room and stood towering over the hapless Dick like an avenging angel.

"I—well—I—" foundered Dick.

"Weren't you watching at all? Didn't you remember how we were to signal if we found Wilson?" Peter was very angry. "Haven't you any brains in your head, for God's sake?" he burst out.

"Peter." Geoffrey had risen. His tone held mild reproof as he came to stand behind the wrathful back of his senior master. He laid a restraining hand on the young man's shoulder. "Just think, Butler. Exactly where did you last see Miss Wayne?"

"I—she was there when we got to the boundary fence, I'm sure. I remember seeing her torch as I climbed over," Dick brought out surlily.

"Well, we know she got that far, then," said Geoffrey. "Peter, you'd better look for her. She may have twisted her ankle or something, or perhaps she's still searching out there. Don't go alone—which of you will go with him?" He looked at the other masters, who all stood up, though Dick was the last to rise. Geoffrey nodded. "Cross, you go," he said. "You others had better get some rest. Don't forget we've got ninety-nine other boys to look after tomorrow. And Peter, make sure Jennifer

219

isn't in the lodge before you start scouring the district."

Peter and Ronald went at once. The others slowly and stiffly collected their raincoats and departed for bed.

Peter and Ronald soon established that Jennifer was not at the lodge. They hurried to the place at the boundary fence where Dick had declared he had seen her.

"She wouldn't have gone back the way we'd just come, if she was still looking for Wilson," said Peter.

"Perhaps she went along the shore. The tide's going out now, she'd know no one had been able to get along that bit of beach by the point before," suggested Ronald.

"I expect that's what she's done," said Peter. "Come on, let's hurry."

They began to scramble along one of the many tracks which ran down that part of the cliff, linking with the path which Christopher had clambered on during his earlier escapade. Presently they reached the beach and began to walk towards the point, which was invisible to them in the blackness of the night. The wind had moderated considerably now, but as it dropped the rain began again. They shouted, and shone their torches about them as they went, until suddenly Peter caught his companion's arm.

"Look, what's that?" he exclaimed.

Ronald blinked into the darkness.

"I can't see anything," he said.

"Up on the cliff there—there's a light, look, by the point." Peter did not wait for Ronald to agree, but began to run towards the base of the cliff where the flickering light could be seen.

Jennifer and Christopher had come to "Fight the Good Fight" by the time Peter could faintly hear their combined voices. The powerful beam of his big torch illuminated them, crouched on their ledge, high up above.

Together Peter and Ronald shouted, and then they heard Jennifer calling, "Peter! Peter! He's here, he's broken his legs."

"We'll go for help. Can you hang on?" yelled Peter, cupping his hands round his mouth.

"All right, but hurry," called Jennifer, and flashed her torch. She clicked the switch again, and the weak light slowly petered out and died.

"Never mind, we'll be safe in no time," she said to the boy.

Peter thought rapidly. Then he decided: "You go to Charnton, Ronald. Get on the road as soon as you can round the point, you might meet a car. There's a chance, if you do, that it will be quicker than going back to school. There's a house anyway at the top of the hill, go and use their phone. I'll go back along the beach to school and ring from there. Hurry!"

Without a word Ronald set off at a loping trot, and Peter began to run back to Arrowhurst.

When the torch expired Christopher began to cry. It was not normal weeping, and Jennifer was alarmed. After a time he grew quiet, and seemed to sleep. She felt panic then, in case weakness overcame him and he began to drift from life. She thought that if he stayed awake his circulation might be stronger, and she tried to rally him. She made him move, and raised him higher against her body, then began to rub his hands again, talking to him and asking him questions. He would not answer, until she said in despair, "Where do you live, Christopher? Tell me about your house," and suddenly he began to talk. She listened then, incredulous with horror, prompting him when his words failed and holding his thin little body close to her for comfort, while the story poured out of him. He finished it as shouts and powerful lights on the cliff above them signalled the arrival of their rescuers.

11

JENNIFER spent the remainder of that night in Charnton Cottage Hospital, but even with the sedatives she had been given sleep was only fitful, and when Peter arrived early the next morning she insisted on returning to school with him.

"I must tell the headmaster what Christopher said last night," she kept saying, near to tears, and in the end Peter agreed to take the responsibility of moving her. Before they left they looked in on Christopher, sleeping behind screens in a corner of the children's ward. His legs had been provisionally set; and he lay, whitefaced, with a bandage round his head and a saline drip connected to his arm. He was weak and exhausted, but though gravely ill the doctors thought he stood a chance of avoiding pneumonia. His head wound was trivial; he was mildly concussed, and the damage to his legs, though extensive, was

224

thought to be less serious than it had at first appeared.

At school, everything on the surface was normal, but the boys sensed the tension of their elders; usually good-natured masters were irritable, and Miss Norton looked as though she had been crying. Jones II found himself something of a hero, since he had been summoned to the head-master's presence the night before, and he disclosed with importance the reason.

"P'rhaps Wilson's dead," said Roberts at breakfast.

"Been murdered, I expect," said Sparrow ghoulishly.

"Miss Norton, is Wilson dead?" asked Roberts loudly, through a mouthful of bread and marmalade.

"No, he is not, and you're not to talk like that," said Phyllis sharply, from her seat at the top of the table.

Roberts stared at her in surprise. She was often strict, but seldom fierce.

"Wilson is ill in bed," she said, and folded her mouth tight shut in an unusually hard line.

Even the insensitive nature of Roberts knew that this was final, and he subsided.

Geoffrey and Marion listened in silence while Jennifer related what Christopher had told her last night. Her story was disconnected, as his had been, with fragments delved from memory and served up without regard for chronology. She spoke of the sheltered, uneventful years Christopher had spent with his grandmother, and then of how he had more lately spent his holidays with his mother. She described the week last year at the seaside, when his mother had seldom spoken to him: how he had been left in the hotel at night not knowing where she was, to have his supper and get to bed on his own. She described the mornings when his mother had never got dressed before twelve, and how he had waited for her, hanging about, fearing to go off by himself in case she wanted him. She told of the life in the London flat, and the breakfasts with Mrs. Davis on the kitchen table. She told of the endless bus rides, the museums, the mornings spent walking round Woolworths and the afternoons at the cinema; and the early banishment to bed before the men arrived. "Different men," said Jennifer shakily. Then she told of the last night of the holidays that had just passed. Sitting on the sofa, wrapped in a rug, Jennifer said:

"'Dirty little snotty-nosed brat, I can't stand the sight of him. He's nothing but a nuisance and I wish to Heaven I could get rid of him.'" The words were etched now for ever in her memory as they had been in Christopher's. When she had said them she began to cry, and Peter, who was sitting beside her on the sofa holding her hand, at once put his arms round her. "He thinks it's because he's always untidy and no good at things, he thinks if he could be good at things and a credit to her she'd like him, that's why the singing meant so much to him," she sobbed. "You can't let her go on treating him like this, you must do something. He can't go back to her," she cried hysterically, while Peter held her closer.

"We will do something," said Geoffrey. "You must go to bed now, Jennifer. You've been splendid. Don't worry any more, just go off to bed." His voice was authoritative, and Jennifer stood up, still holding Peter's sleeve.

"I'm so sorry," she sniffed, mopping

her eyes with the handkerchief in her other hand.

"That's all right, my dear," said Marion. "You're tired out. Now come along." She took Jennifer's arm, and reluctantly the girl let go of Peter.

"Peter will come and see you when you've had a good sleep, and not before," said Marion firmly. She led her from the room and off up to the sickroom, where she was to remain under the eye of Matron until she had recovered from the events of the night before.

"What a business," said Geoffrey, sinking into a chair as the women left.

"Awful," said Peter.

"I suppose the boy was right? Jennifer couldn't have dreamed all that, could she?" wondered Geoffrey.

"Good heavens, no, you couldn't invent it," cried Peter. "Besides, having met the woman several times, I'd believe her capable of almost anything," he added grimly.

"It's possible, I agree," said Geoffrey.

"That poor little blighter," said Peter. "Think of it: struggling along, hoping to be a success to make her like him. You wouldn't think a child could go on caring about someone who treated him like that, would you?"

"He probably doesn't really care for her, but he's trying to convince himself that he does, because it's usual to love one's mother," said Geoffrey. "He feels he must defend her, even to himself."

"Sort of loyal 'my country right or wrong,' eh?" said Peter. "God, to think I imagined all his trouble was just homesickness! I'll never make a schoolmaster, Geoff."

"You don't do so badly," said Geoffrey. "'By our pupils we are taught.' I'm going to get on to the old lady, the grandmother. She'll have to deal with this."

At nine o'clock that night Jennifer woke up to find Peter sitting in a chair beside her bed. She smiled at him, drowsily, and he leaned forward and said, "Hullo, Jenny."

"Peter," she murmured, and blinked, while the crowded happenings of the past forty-eight hours came back to her. She had roused earlier to eat a large lunch, and Matron had woken her at half-past seven for supper, but each time she had dropped straight off to sleep again as soon as she had eaten.

"What time is it?" she asked.

"It's nine o'clock," he said. "You have had a good sleep."

They looked at each other, suddenly shy and tongue-tied, until Jennifer said, "How's Christopher?"

"He's much better, he's slept all day, like you, and he's stronger now," said Peter. "I saw him for a few minutes this evening. They think he'll be all right."

"What about his legs?" she asked then.

"They'll have to be properly set in a day or two, when he's strong enough. They don't seem to be unduly worried about it. He's broken a few ribs, too, but not to matter," Peter told her.

"I was afraid he might lose a leg," said Jennifer. "I had to pull them straight, to get his wet clothes off."

"The doctors said that if he avoids pneumonia it will be entirely thanks to you for doing that," said Peter robustly. "Apart, also, from the little matter of your saving his life. There's no reason why he shouldn't be perfectly well in a couple of months. Children are frightfully tough, you know. But Jenny, what about you?" He looked at her anxiously. "How do you feel?"

"Very, very lazy," she said, snuggling down into her bed.

"Go to sleep again," he said.

"Not now," she answered, and blushed.

He moved towards her, awkwardly, and then he was holding her hands in his and kissing them, and they were both half laughing.

"Oh, Jenny, I nearly went out of my mind when you were lost," he said, and his brown eyes were dark as he remembered his fears.

She smiled. "You won't get rid of me so easily," she said dreamily. "Wasn't it funny, I knew it was you when I saw the torches. I never thought of it being anybody else."

"Jenny, darling Jenny," he said softly. Her eyes were on his: they looked enormous in her pale face. "Buck up and get well," he said gently. Then he sat back in his chair, still holding her hand, and as she closed her eyes again Peter knew that the barriers of reserve remaining between them had all dissolved.

He was still sitting there, holding her hand, an hour later when Phyllis came in with a glass of hot milk.

"Gracious, Peter, are you still here? Have you forgotten that this building is full of impressionable schoolboys? Be off at once," she scolded.

Peter grinned. "They're all asleep," he said, getting up. "You were young once, Phyl, and not so long ago either." He seized her round the waist and hugged her. "I saw Dr. Hunt making sheep's eyes at you today, you can't deceive me."

"Peter, you need six of the best with your own cane," said Phyllis. "I don't know why you put up with him, Jenny."

Jennifer smiled. "He's really quite nice," she said. "He just takes a bit of getting used to."

"Peter, say goodnight to our heroine and get out," said Phyllis firmly. "I'm going to fetch a fresh hot-water bottle for her, and if you're still here when I get back I shall send for the headmaster."

She went away, and the two young people began to laugh.

"I'd better go," said Peter. "It will soon be tomorrow. Bless you, Jenny, I do love you so."

"Goodnight, Peter," said Jennifer, softly, and then, with an effort, "Darling!" She looked at him solemnly, round-eyed at her own daring, and he bent and touched her lips in the lightest and most tender of kisses. Then he was gone.

12

CHRISTOPHER said, "Sir, I suppose I'll have to have six of the best again?"

He was sitting up in bed, very pale, with both legs in plaster casts before him, and his ribs strapped up. A band of sticking plaster had replaced the bandage over the wound on his head.

Peter's mouth twitched.

"Well, not this time, Wilson. I think we'll let you off." he said gravely.

"Sir, I didn't mean to do it, I didn't mean to go. I wasn't running away," Christopher burst out. Since his ordeal he seemed to have a great desire for speech, and had developed a new articulacy.

The further nightmare that had been haunting Jennifer and Peter receded. Standing one on each side of the patient's bed, they exchanged glances. Christopher had today been brought grandly back to school in an ambulance, and now lay in splendour, the sole occupant of the sickroom, with the remains of a celebratory tea surrounding him.

"I mean, I don't know why I went to Charnton, and then I thought I'd better get back as soon as I could, so I went along the beach and the tide came in," he explained earnestly.

"I know, old chap. You were a mutt to forget about the tide, but you won't again," said Peter mildly.

"I'd promised not to go out of school," Christopher insisted, bent on attrition.

Peter waited to see what would follow. The small boy looked quickly at Jennifer, and then back at Peter again. He swallowed, and then went on:

"You see, I was a bit cheesed at my mater not coming, and I thought I'd meet her," he said determinedly. "I forgot the London road doesn't go through Charnton. I really promise not to do it again, sir, cross my heart and hope to die, but perhaps I'd better have six of the best to make sure." He watched Peter steadily from wide, anxious brown eyes.

Peter said, for some admonition would not now be superfluous, "You realise we were all very worried about you? Everyone was looking for you, and the police too."

"Yes, I do." Christopher looked abashed. "I'm very sorry."

"Well, then, you've promised never to do it again, so we'll say no more about it," said Peter. "But you do realise, don't you, what a lot of harm can come just from thoughtlessness?"

But whose thoughtlessness? was in his mind. Surely in this instance Janine, not her son, was the culprit.

"Yes, sir," said Christopher, promptly.

"Well, then, that's that," said Peter with relief. "Now how about some more cake?"

Jennifer looked at them both.

"You've got lots to talk about," she said. "I'll leave you to it. Goodbye, Christopher. I'm glad you're back, we've missed you." She kissed him in a most unschoolmistress-like manner and went away.

Christopher watched her go. Then he sighed.

"Miss Wayne's very nice, as ladies go," he said profoundly.

"Er—yes," Peter agreed. "She is."

"Men are better, though," said Christopher. "They keep their word."

"Ladies usually do, too," said Peter. He removed the bed-table with its load of crumby plates and empty cup that covered Christopher's chest and sat down on the end of the bed.

When there was no answer to this simple statement, he asked, "Do you remember much about that night on the cliff?"

Christopher shook his head.

"No, sir. Isn't it funny, I don't remember any of it, only climbing up and slipping, and then I remember Miss Wayne was there, but not if she said anything."

"You don't remember singing, 'Onward, Christian Soldiers'?"

"No, sir. Did we?" Christopher looked astonished.

"You did. It was a good way to keep cheerful while you waited to be rescued," said Peter. "Well, never mind."

"I'm afraid I must have been a nuisance, sir," said Christopher, with magnificent understatement. "Mother always says I am one, but I don't mean to be," he added, in a matter-of-fact voice. "I won't be able to go home for the holidays, will I, sir? My legs won't be better in time." A wide smile spread over his features as he said this.

Peter stared at him, and then comprehension dawned.

"We'll have to see what the doctor says," he replied evasively. "Your legs will take quite a time to mend, but you needn't think you're going to lie here in luxury while they do. You'll be riding around in a smart wheel-chair in a few days and doing lessons like everyone else, and when your ribs are better you'll probably be able to hobble about a bit."

"Will I?" asked Christopher. "A wheel-chair? Who'll push?"

Peter laughed. "You may be able to work it yourself," he said. "Otherwise I expect your friend Jones II will oblige. I've told him he can come and see you this evening for half an hour. He'll be here soon. He's got some new insects to show you. Don't let him drop them into your bed."

Christopher made a face. "Jones does love beetles," he said regretfully. "I prefer stamps myself. Do you think I could start a collection, sir? Peterson has a lovely lot. I think it would be fun."

"That's a good idea, Wilson," Peter approved. "I've got a few you can have to start you off, and I believe I've got an old album somewhere. I'll look it out for you."

"Oh, thank you, sir," said Christopher. He leaned back against his pillows, suddenly tired.

"You have a little nap till Jones comes," said Peter. He patted the narrow shoulder. "Goodnight, Wilson," he said.

Christopher smiled. "Goodnight, sir," he said. "And thanks awfully."

Peter went away. As he went downstairs he turned over in his mind the problem that was Christopher. What a difference there was in him now: although he was still pale and hollow-cheeked, he had quite lost the prematurely old look that had made him so different from the other boys, and become just another little nine-year-old. He purged himself to Jennifer that night, Peter thought. It was an odd but merciful quirk of nature that had wiped away all memory of his confidences.

He wondered what would happen about the holidays. Probably the old grandmother would arrange for him to go to Cumberland and stay with his cousins when she had heard Geoffrey's story.

But the next morning Geoffrey called Peter into his study after breakfast and handed him, without comment, a letter to read. It was written in spiky writing on a single sheet of paper, and came from Christopher's aunt.

"Dear Mr. Frost," Peter read. "I am writing to tell you that my mother died peacefully last night. She never regained consciousness from the stroke she had the day before you telephoned about Christopher's accident, and so she never knew what had happened to him. I am glad that her mind was not troubled at the last by problems she could do nothing to solve.

"Please break the sad news to Christopher when you consider he is well enough to hear it. He was very fond of his grandmother, and I am afraid it will be a shock to him. His cousins and all of us are deeply saddened by our loss, but my mother had been failing for some time and we draw comfort from knowing that she was spared prolonged suffering. She hated the limitations ill-health had forced upon her, and would have found it hard to endure an existence as a complete invalid.

"I am sure that with your experience you will be able to sort out with Christopher whatever small worry it was you wanted to discuss with my mother. Yours sincerely, Freda McNair."

"Well!" Peter handed the letter back to Geoffrey. "Poor old lady, how sad," he said.

"A merciful release, I imagine," said Geoffrey. "But it doesn't help us. Now what do we do?"

Peter turned and began to walk up and down the room, stroking his chin thoughtfully.

"Goodness knows," he said. "We'll have to do something that's certain. The boy said last night with a beaming smile that he wouldn't be well enough to go home for the holidays."

"Did you tell him he would be?" asked Geoffrey.

"I hedged," said Peter. "I thought you'd probably fix up something with the old lady. Do you think the aunt—this Mrs. McNair—would have him?"

"I daresay, but she hasn't offered her help. His mother has custody of him, I imagine, and it's a bit tricky to go over her head to Mrs. McNair. The old lady was different."

"Surely the situation is serious enough to warrant it?" said Peter.

"I don't know," said Geoffrey. He went to look out of the window while he cogitated; he did not want to become involved in the affairs of the Wilson family. Peter turned to pace the room again, frowning, and just then Marion entered the room. She looked cool and elegant in a green dress, with her hair gleaming like an autumn chestnut.

"Hullo! What are you two looking so glum about?" she asked. "Peter, for goodness' sake don't prowl like a caged panther, you're wearing a track in the carpet."

"Sorry," said Peter. He halted by the window.

"We are glum," said Geoffrey. "Old Mrs. Wilson has left us with the problem of her grandson."

"Poor old soul. Still, I was expecting it, weren't you?" Marion said. "It sounded as if she was very ill."

"No, I wasn't," said Geoffrey. "I hoped she'd recover and lend us a hand with the boy."

"I don't see what she could have done," said Marion.

"She could have gone and pi-jawed her daughter-in-law," said Geoffrey.

"It wouldn't have had any effect," said Marion. "I imagine she'd given that up years ago. But I don't think she can have had any idea of what sort of person Janine Dufay is, or she wouldn't have let the child go to her."

"If she's got the custody of him, she's entitled to have him," Peter pointed out.

"Yes, but has she?" asked Marion.

"Anyone less suitable to have custody of a child than Mrs. Wilson would be hard to find," said Geoffrey.

"This all throws rather a different light on that ogre Mr. Wilson, doesn't it?" said Marion, still pursuing her own line of thought. "We never really heard what had happened, did we? It was all over and settled long before the child came here."

The men did not answer. Neither of them had been listening. Peter said abruptly, "You'll have to go and see her, won't you, Geoff? Mrs. Wilson, I mean."

"I'm beginning to be afraid I may," said Geoffrey. "Unless we just leave it for a bit, and hope it sorts itself out," he suggested hopefully. "This Mrs. McNair may think of some idea, when she's had time to get over her mother's death."

"You can't leave it!" Peter and Marion both spoke together.

"No, Geoffrey, this is a time when we've got to interfere," said Marion definitely. "The child is our responsibility, after all. It's criminal that his mother should behave like that. She can have her boy-friends, all well and good, if she must, but not when Christopher's there."

"What about Peter going?" said Geoffrey, seeking any escape from an undertaking that he felt himself totally unable to handle. "Yes, that's an idea, Peter. You're senior master and allowed to give beatings. I depute you to do this. It will add to your experience."

Peter looked appalled.

"You can't do that, Geoffrey, and you

know it," said Marion firmly. "You're still headmaster, and this is something you've got to do yourself. Besides, Peter's too young to cope with it."

"We're all too young to cope with that creature," said Geoffrey. "But I suppose you're right. It seems the only thing to do. What a woman! She's never rung up once to enquire for the child."

"I don't think she's written to him, or sent him a single parcel," said Marion, taking a cigarette from the box, and tapping it on the desk.

Peter held a light for her.

"Thanks, Peter." Marion blew funnels of smoke down her nostrils. "I know I grumble at Mrs. Jones for ringing up whenever one of her sons so much as sneezes, but far better that than sheer, callous indifference like this. Phyllis or I have written a note to her every day, as we always do when anyone's not well, but I doubt if she's troubled to look at them." She got off the desk where she had been sitting, and moved over to the mantelpiece. "What will you do, Geoff? Get her on the telephone and make an appointment?"

"Yes, if I can get through," said Geoffrey. "It's no good writing. As you say, I doubt if she'd read it, much less answer."

"Perhaps she won't see you," said Peter.

"Oh, yes, she will," Marion prophesied. "Geoffrey's a man."

Marion's psychology was correct, and Janine agreed, when at last located on the telephone, to see Geoffrey the next afternoon. Accordingly he set off by the lunchtime train to London, dressed in his new dark grey suit, and looking, as Marion told him when he departed, more like a prosperous stockbrocker than a beggarly usher.

His thoughts as he stood in the lift being magically transported aloft to the door of Janine's flat were not cheerful. He rehearsed a few opening sentences in his mind, but was unresolved how best to begin the conversation when the lift stopped, and he was compelled to leave it and walk across a thickly-carpeted landing to Flat 10.

Janine opened the door immediately upon his ring, catching him straightening his tie and smoothing his hair with his hand for all the world like one of his own schoolboys.

"Well, Mr. Frost—or may I call you Geoffrey now that we're such old friends," she purred, ushering him in and leading the way to her sitting-room. "This is nice."

She wore a sleeveless dress in apricot silk, and to Geoffrey's alarmed eyes there seemed to be a great deal of peach-like Janine showing round the edges. She offered him a cigarette from a box full of Turkish, and as he declined one he noticed a smear of lipstick along the neckline of her dress where the material had brushed against her painted mouth. He frowned in distaste. Such an accident would never befall the fastidious Marion.

Janine waved him to a chair as she fixed her own cigarette into a jade holder, and he sat down primly on the edge of it, not daring to relax. She then cast herself full-length upon the sofa opposite, and smiled invitingly at him.

"What brings you to London?" she asked. She was used to paving the way. "I thought you couldn't bear to tear yourself away from all that cricket." Her voice was penetrating and very distinct; part of her career, Geoffrey supposed vaguely.

He suppressed a mad impulse to say, in answer to her question, "British Railways," and tried to pull himself together.

"I came to see you," he began carefully. His palms were sweating; life had not often washed Geoffrey up in such situations, and though some of the parents were difficult no other Arrowhurst boy had ever had a mother quite like this. He reminded himself firmly that he was at least fifteen years older than she, and should therefore be more than competent to conduct an interview with her.

But: "Oh, how lovely of you," Janine said, opening her blue eyes very widely.

"About Christopher," he persevered.

"Oh!" The childish face fell, and she pouted. "Silly child, I hope he hasn't been getting into any more mischief."

"No, Mrs. Wilson. He won't be able to do anything like that for a long time," Geoffrey told her firmly. Control and confidence returned to him. "He is getting on very well now, but I doubt if you realise quite how ill he has been."

"Oh—pooh!" Janine dismissed this

with a wave of her hand. "Children soon recover."

"Fortunately they do. Even delicate boys like Christopher have remarkable powers of recovery," said Geoffrey.

"Christopher isn't delicate," said Janine.

"He's not robust, and he's very sensitive," said Geoffrey. "Mrs. Wilson, my task today in speaking to you is not easy. I am here because I am responsible for your son while he is at school, and we have noticed this term that he has been under extreme nervous strain." The phrase he had composed in the lift now rolled grandiloquently off his tongue, leaving his mind thereafter blank, and he paused.

Janine looked sulky. "Hasn't he had his corners rubbed off yet?" she asked in a bored voice. "Why worry me about it? That's your job. Goodness knows I pay you enough to do it." She examined her long red finger-nails, dropping ash unheeded from her cigarette as she did so. Geoffrey felt nauseated: her hands were like the predatory claws of some vulture bird. In spite of himself he glanced at her slim legs; they were stockingless, and the skin looked very white and smooth; crimson toenails protruded through the thongs of her high-heeled sandals.

Geoffrey swallowed, and plunged on with determination.

"Mrs. Wilson, Christopher is devoted to you, as I am sure you know. He was very disappointed when you did not come to the school concert, and that was why he had the accident."

"Don't be ridiculous," said Janine. The afternoon was not going according to her expectations: very different had been her ideas.

Geoffrey grew angry at last.

"Mrs. Wilson, please listen to me," he said, in the tones that could subdue a hundred yelling schoolboys. "Whether you like what I am saying or not, you must understand. You did not come to the concert: Christopher waited for you with the other boys, and when you did not arrive he set out to meet you. He went the wrong way, and when he realised this he started to come back to school along the beach. He forgot about the tides, and got cut off, so he started to climb the cliff. He fell, breaking both his legs and three ribs, and concussing himself. He was missing for a long time, and was only found after the police and my staff had searched for hours. He owes his life to the fact that one of our young mistresses climbed down the cliff to him, and gave him first-aid till help came."

"I know all that—you told me on the telephone," said Janine pettishly.

"Mrs. Wilson, why didn't you come to the concert?" asked Geoffrey, sweeping on. "Surely you could have sent a message if you were unavoidably prevented? Children do attach so much importance to things that may seem very trivial to us, and this mattered a great deal to your boy."

"I forgot about it," said Janine. "Anyway, it would have been very boring. It seems to me that you don't keep a very good watch on the boys if you let them escape like that," she added.

Geoffrey said: "I admit that we may have been at fault in not noticing Christopher's absence immediately, but he was missed within half an hour of his leaving the school. The boys are constantly supervised; there is always at least one master on duty whatever they are doing, but on that day every boy was supposed to be either in the gym watching the concert, or else performing in it, and every boy but Christopher *was* there. It meant a lot to him that you should hear him sing, and he was sure you would keep your promise to come."

Janine had been fidgeting during this peroration; her face grew steadily more sulky, and her lips drooped. As she appeared unable to think of a riposte Geoffrey felt he was at last making headway, and hastened to follow up his advantage.

"Last holidays Christopher overheard a remark you made to someone who was visiting you which led him to imagine that you did not care for him," he continued. "No doubt he misunderstood what you said, but it seems it has been on his mind all this term. We thought he was home-sick, and we only discovered the real trouble when he told Miss Wayne about it on the night of the accident. I don't have to tell you, I'm sure, how vital it is for children to feel secure, and it is a tragedy for any child to assume he is unwanted, however mistaken the assumption. I am certain you will be anxious to put this mistake right with Christopher."

But he knew it was not a mistake as she stared at him, with eyes gone hard, like blue stones, in her perfect little face.

"What did he overhear?" she asked in a voice like ice.

Geoffrey could not bring himself to repeat what Jennifer had said.

"He heard you say you wished you could get rid of him," he replied.

In one feline movement Janine sprang from the sofa. She remembered the night at the end of the holidays.

"Why, the eavesdropping little beast," she cried, standing tense over Geoffrey and clenching her hands like talons.

"He didn't mean to listen, Mrs. Wilson," said Geoffrey, also rising, and moving quickly behind the chair so that it separated them.

"Of course he did, he's always hanging about in corners, the lying little sneak," she said viciously. "What was he doing outside the door if he wasn't listening, tell me that?"

"Going to the bathroom, I imagine,"

said Geoffrey promptly, feeling better now that he was on his feet and topping her by one more. "But be that as it may, he heard or thought he heard you use those words, and now he thinks you don't want him. He has been trying to win your approval by his achievements at school. Won't you let him feel he has succeeded, Mrs. Wilson? He doesn't get many letters; couldn't you write to him, or better still, come down and see him? And make him welcome in the holidays?"

Blind rage now motivated Janine. Her doll-like prettiness had vanished from her pink and white miniature of a face.

"How dare you!" she seethed. But for Christopher, Henry might have married her: he had disappeared now from her life in the disconcerting way that most of her men did, just as she hoped for permanency. Fury that Geoffrey had not now succumbed to her charms but instead had admonished her lashed her on, and drove away the remnants of her self-control.

"You're not fit to have a school!" she stormed, stamping her small foot. "How dare you come here insulting me like this!" She cast about her for ammunition to hurl against the unfortunate Geoffrey who watched her in dismay. Nothing in his life before had prepared him for an encounter with a virago. "Your school's no good—you let the boys fall down cliffs—you come here spreading lies and slander!" Suddenly she remembered Peter Farquhar, the young master who also had resisted her and who had not even used the ticket she had sent him for her play. Christopher's letters, which occasionally she read for lack of anything better to do, were always full of his name. "You and that other master—Mr. Farquhar—you're much too interested in Christopher—it isn't right—he's always on about him—there's something unhealthy about it. Your school's a disgrace—you employ men who—"

"Mrs. Wilson, please!" Geoffrey, appalled and unable to believe the evidence of his ears, interrupted her before in her deplorable exhibition she uttered the frighful accusation that was springing to her tongue. "Remember what you are saying!"

"I know what I'm saying!" cried Janine, now past the point of no return. "I'm saying that Christopher will be leaving your school, and I shall make no secret of the reason. Now you'd better go. I've no more time to waste with you."

Geoffrey opened his mouth to speak, but she stood glaring at him like a small fury, and he knew no words of his would calm her now. If he said anything else she might indeed carry out what he took to be her idle threat and remove Christopher from school: that would, he was sure, be the worst calamity that could now befall the child. He allowed himself to be driven out of the door and into the passage, and was soon once again in the lift dejectedly descending to street level. His spirits were at zero in the train returning to Charnton; he would have done less harm by staying at home.

Janine, left alone, paced the floor for a few minutes. Then, to restore her wounded self-esteem, she picked up the telephone. She drew blank at the first number that she dialled, and again at the second. Finally, in despair, she telephoned the pub near Arrowhurst where Dick Butler bought his cigarettes, and left a message for him. She knew that he would salve her damaged pride and smooth her ruffled feathers; and he did more.

13

CHRISTOPHER frowned intently over the map of New Zealand that was pinned to a drawing board across his knees. He scribbled industriously with a green crayon, blocking in the low-lying land. Already chocolate mountains occupied much space, and vivid rivers wandered doubtfully about like errant threads of cotton. At last he could think of no more natural relief to add: North and South Islands faced one another across a violent blue strait. He sat back in the wheel-chair and lowered the board on to his plastered legs. He was parked beside the end desk in the front row of Form II, too close for choice to the eagle eye of Ronald Cross who presided over the Geography lesson.

The bell rang, Ronald collected the papers, and the little boys spilled into noisy chatter like starlings into the autumn sky. Christopher set off in his chair to pursue the departing form of the master, calling: "Sir, sir, please!"

"Yes, Wilson, what is it?" Ronald turned, his pile of books under his arm, and looked enquiringly at the eager face turned up to him.

"Sir, please can I have your autograph on my legs?" Christopher asked. "Look, I've got almost all the other masters, and nearly all the boys too," he said with pride.

Obediently Ronald scrutinised the plasters. No longer snowy-white, both legs were covered with ink and pencil scrawls.

"Gracious, Wilson, what a collection," he exclaimed, producing his famous dual colour pen. "Which would you like, red or green?" he asked.

"Oh, green please, or a bit of both," said Christopher. "I've got lots of red already."

"Hm. 'Instead of a boot I'm on Wilson's old foot, D. Jones,'" read Ronald, with difficulty. "Well, Jones, I never knew you were a poet."

"I can often think of rhymes," Jones declared, with great want of modesty. "Actually, that one went rather bish."

"Well, you aren't the first poet to take a bit of licence," said Ronald with a chuckle. He paused in solemn thought, watched by an interested audience of small boys; after suitable reflection he wrote with a flourish, in appropriate colours:

"Red for stop, green for go,
Please don't bump this big toe."

"Oh, jolly good, sir, thanks awfully!" said Christopher gratefully, wriggling the naked toes that protruded from his plaster.

"What do you think of that for a rhyme, Jones?" asked Ronald. "Not too good, is it? They don't always rhyme if they're spelt the same."

"Like 'plough' and 'rough'," said Jones keenly, showing his appreciation of the literary turn to the discussion.

"And 'dough' and 'cough'," added Ronald. "I say, Wilson, you have got a good collection," he went on, busy reading the further admonitions that covered Christopher's legs.

"' Drive carefully, 'twould be disaster

If you should crack this handsome
    plaster.
A. Hunt, Physician-in-Chief'," he
    saw, and

"' A beating will be hard to give
While in this chair you're forced to
    live,'" signed
by Phyllis.

Wilfrid Fitzgibbon had drawn a neat
sketch of the wheel-chair and its occupant
careering along at speed, with matron, her
cap flying, in hot pursuit, and initialled it
with a flowing monogram.

"I say, these are fun," exclaimed Ronald
with enthusiasm. "I shall read the rest of
them this afternoon at the match. Mind
you don't go smashing them up before
then."

Whistling under his breath he strode
away, and Christopher, with his companions followed. His chair was in the
centre of a group of noisy little boys, and
he himself was quite the noisiest, entirely
absorbed in shouting down Sparrow who
had betted he could run faster along the
tiled passage than Christopher could bowl

in his chair; and he was at long last occupied only with what concerned him at the moment, without thought for past or future, as all small boys should be.

At lunch, he was an object of envy when he propelled himself into the dining-room and up to a vacant space at the corner table. Most of the boys thought it looked super-duper to be in a chair, as long as you weren't to be there for ever, and Christopher was the only seated person while Geoffrey said Grace over the heads of the company.

With a crashing sound as of thunder the ninety-nine other boys pulled out their chairs and sat down to demolish platefuls of cold beef and salad.

To Christopher's mortification he was made to rest in bed for most of the afternoon, but at half-past three matron got him up, and Phyllis came to wheel him over the garden to the cricket pitch. She parked him beside a crowd of his friends under the shade of the tall trees at the edge of the field.

"There, Wilson, now you can drive yourself about if you want to," she said, setting the brake on his chair. Although his eyes were still enormous in his thin face there was some colour now in his cheeks.

"Thanks awfully, Miss Norton," he said cheerfully. "I say, look what Mr. Cross wrote on my plaster this morning. Jolly good, wouldn't you say?"

Phyllis bent and duly appreciated Ronald's poetic flight.

"I can't decide which is best," said Christopher with a frown. "I like the drawings, don't you?"

Phyllis said: "I specially like the one of you tearing along with matron chasing you. Who did that? Mr. Fitzgibbon, was it?" She peered at the flourishing intertwined initials drawn in violet ink.

"Yes. It's just like matron, isn't it?" said Christopher.

"Just like," Phyllis agreed, with a smile.

"I've got Dan Dare, too," said Christopher, squinting at his leg like a connoisseur at an art gallery, "and Davy Crockett, and the Saint, and a horse, and a cat, and lots of aeroplanes—see, a Delta wing—and that's a space rocket."

"I didn't know we had so many artists at Arrowhurst," said Phyllis.

"Do you think Mr. Frost would do something? He's the only master I haven't got," Christopher said, "except Mr. Butler, of course."

"I'm sure Mr. Frost will sign if you ask him, and Mr. Butler too," said Phyllis.

"I'll just ask Mr. Frost," said Christopher quickly.

"Why leave out Mr. Butler?" Phyllis asked, in mild surprise. "Won't you hurt his feelings?"

"Oh, that's just his hard cheese," said Christopher perfunctorily.

Phyllis glanced sharply at the invalid, who looked embarrassed and said quickly: "Do you think I could go and ask Mr. Frost now? Is he too busy?"

"No, I'm sure he's not," said Phyllis, abandoning the curiosity she felt at this revelation of Dick's unpopularity. "I'll come with you and give you a push if you get becalmed."

Christopher set off, and she walked beside his chair, helping him unobtrusively over the grass. Everyone was fearful of spoiling Christopher, which their inclinations made them prone to do; but he was so cheerful and courageous that it was not hard to encourage him to be independent.

"Hullo, Wilson! My goodness, you look comfortable," said Marion, as Christopher drove his chariot up in style to the front of the pavilion.

He grinned at her.

"How are the autographs getting on? Mr. Cross has been telling me all about them," said Geoffrey.

"Oh, very well, sir, but I haven't got yours. Please could I have it, sir?" asked Christopher.

"Certainly, if I can find a vacant inch," said Geoffrey, surveying the area of leg available. "It's no good putting it behind your heel or you won't be able to read it. You won't be short of light reading, anyway, Wilson, while you've got all this to look at. Pity to lose it when your plasters come off, eh?"

"I think you'll have to write them all down in a book and keep them," said Marion. "You could trace the drawings off, couldn't you?"

"Oh yes, so I could," said Christopher. "That's a good idea."

"Now what shall I write?" mused

264

Geoffrey, unscrewing his Parker 51. "You've got quite a bit of Latin, I see, and even some Greek." He frowned, trying without his glasses to decipher the tags and maxims freely scrawled. "Do you understand them all, Wilson?"

Christopher looked sheepish. "Most of them, I think sir," he said doubtfully.

Geoffrey smiled. "Well, I'll stick to English," he said, and wrote "Time and tide stayeth for no man" in his neat, scholarly writing. "Don't forget that," he added.

Christopher blushed, but he saw that Geoffrey still smiled.

"Thanks awfully, sir," he said.

Marion took the pen from Geoffrey's hand.

"I refuse to be left out of this," she said, choosing a place by Christopher's left knee between a skull and crossbones and a facsimile of "Harris Tweed, Special Agent." She drew the silhouette, rear view, of a seated cat, and signed it. "I'm afraid that's the only thing I can draw," she said, adding whiskers to the sides of the head, and a curling tail below.

"It's supersonic," said Christopher,

bestowing the highest praise in his vocabulary. "Thanks awfully, Mrs. Frost."

He wheeled himself rapidly away, and the others watched his zigzag progress as he hurried back towards Jones II and his friends.

"He's looking much better," Geoffrey said.

"Yes, he's getting on well," said Phyllis. "Alec had a look at him this afternoon and was very pleased."

"Oh, I didn't know he was coming in today," said Marion. "Who else is laid low? I didn't think there was anyone in the sickroom."

"There isn't anyone," said Phyllis. "It was for Bedford's polio injection. As he lives so near it came under Alec's jurisdiction. I'd forgotten it was today till matron reminded me at lunch."

"There are two to go home for theirs next week, aren't there?" said Geoffrey. "What a nuisance all these things are. Don't forget them, will you, Phyl?"

Have I ever? she longed to ask, but refrained. It was unlike Geoffrey to grumble about the petty tiresomenesses that were legion in his life. Boys were constantly being whisked off by their parents to pet dentists and chiropodists, causing much disruption to their scholastic programme; and the polio injections became available only in the districts where the children had been registered for them.

"It's rather bad luck on Wilson being the only one up in the sickroom," said Marion. "I wonder if he'd be better back in his dormitory with the others?"

"I think he would, when he's a bit stronger," said Phyllis. "But a bit of peace and quiet and early bed will do him no harm for a few more days. He still tires very quickly."

"He's quite a hero now," said Marion, looking across at the grey and green figures sprawling about on the grass. "He doesn't deserve to be."

"Oh, I don't know," said Phyllis. "It wasn't really his fault, and he's being awfully good. It must be wretched to be plastered up like that in this hot weather."

"Perhaps he won't be so patient when the novelty wears off," said Marion.

"What's happening about the holidays?" Phyllis asked.

"We haven't heard a word since my disastrous interview with his mother," said Geoffrey, breaking his long silence. "We'll just have to hope things will go better. She probably will be more discreet."

"Poor boy," said Phyllis. "It seems all wrong that he should have to go there. Don't you think you should get in touch with the aunt?"

"I don't think we can let ourselves become involved," said Geoffrey. "I'm hoping Mrs. Wilson will forget her threat to take him away. I'm sure it was just idle rhetoric—her tongue ran away with her— and I feel our best course is to keep quiet and trust that things will simmer down."

"'Don't worry, it may never happen,' that's your view, is it?" asked Marion.

Geoffrey nodded.

Phyllis frowned, and was about to speak when a sudden ripple of applause from the spectators drew their attention back to the match. Jones I had caught the opposing captain, holding a very difficult ball as he fell flat on the grass with his arm in the air.

"Where's Peter this afternoon?" asked Marion, when the excitement was over and the new enemy batsman in his mustard-coloured cap had walked out from the pavilion.

"He's umpiring after tea," said Geoffrey. "He said something about taking the non-swimmers down for a second bathe as it's so warm."

"Here he comes now," said Phyllis.

Peter was walking rapidly towards them from the direction of the school buildings.

"He looks as if he's in a hurry," she went on, and as he reached them, said: "You look as if you'd all the world on your shoulders, Peter. Sit down and rest yourself."

Peter did not reply directly. He said, addressing Geoffrey: "Mrs. Wilson's here. She's been saying some frightful things. You must come and see her, Geoffrey."

Geoffrey rose at once. "I'll come," he said, and the two men without another word went back towards the house.

"Well!" said Phyllis. "That was most informative."

Marion watched the figure of her husband disappear. Her face wore a quizzical look. Then she said abruptly: "I'm going too."

"Can't they cope?" asked Phyllis, lazily.

"I'm not sure, and I want to hear what happens," said Marion, getting up. She looked down at Phyllis who was reclining, not very elegantly, in a deck chair. "Has Geoffrey told you the full story of his interview the other day?"

"Not in detail," Phyllis said. "I know she threatened to take the child away, of course, but I don't suppose she meant it, as Geoffrey said just now."

"He didn't tell you what she said about Peter?"

"No!" Phyllis looked startled.

"Well, I will," said Marion, and did.

"Now I'm going to see what's happening in the drawing-room," she ended, and set off with determination. As her tall, slight figure walked quickly away over the grass Phyllis was left staring after her, open-mouthed, in horrified unbelief.

14

JANINE was looking less like a doll and more like an angry woman. She wore a tight-fitting flowered silk dress with a wide, square neckline, and a small white hat on the back of her blonde head. On her feet were her usual stilt-heeled shoes, pale blue, just the colour of her eyes. As usual she smoked a cigarette in jerky puffs, this time through a long ivory holder.

She was standing by the fireplace, where a vase of tall delphiniums filled the empty grate, and she turned slowly as Geoffrey and Peter entered through the french window.

"Good afternoon," said Geoffrey firmly, walking into the room.

Janine did not reply. She stared at him for a moment, consideringly.

"Where is Christopher?" she said at last, and to Peter: "I asked you to fetch him."

"Please repeat to Mr. Frost what you

have been saying to me," said Peter levelly. A pulse showed in his lean cheek, but otherwise he appeared calm.

"Mr. Frost already knows my views," said Janine, flicking ash all over Marion's carpet.

"You were upset when we met, I'm sure you spoke hastily," interposed Geoffrey swiftly.

"I was not in the least upset." Janine spoke coldly. "This school is not a fit place for any boy, and I have come to take Christopher away now."

"But the boy isn't well—he needs care and attention. How do you plan to look after him?" demanded Geoffrey.

"That's my business," said Janine.

"Mrs. Wilson, I beg you to reconsider." Geoffrey strove for patience. "At least think things over till the end of the term. Christopher has settled down now, and a change would be very hard on him."

"There is no question of thinking things over when you employ masters like Mr. Farquhar," said Janine, glaring at Peter with eyes like pebbles.

"And what has Peter done?" enquired Marion superbly, stepping into the room.

Peter just looked at her. He could not bring himself to use the words, and glanced at Geoffrey in despair. Janine, however, had no such inhibitions, and bluntly made her accusation in a few words.

"Mrs. Wilson, please take care," said Geoffrey. "What you are saying is quite impossible. Mr. Farquhar has been here for years; he is my senior master and the most trusted member of my staff."

"Then you're a fool," said Janine. "I can prove what I say."

Marion came forward. She stood in front of Janine and regarded her steadily.

"You realise you can be taken to Court for slander?" she asked.

"It will be Mr. Farquhar who will be taken to Court," said Janine. "Fetch Dick Butler. He will bear out what I say."

The others looked startled. Marion took a grip on herself.

"Very well," she said, and rang the bell. They waited in silence, until the maid, in her green overall, appeared.

"Please find Mr. Butler and ask him to come here," said Marion. "He's probably up on the cricket field."

"Yes, madam." The maid withdrew, and the four remained, standing where they were, silent. Then Geoffrey moved across the room to Peter's side. Marion continued to stare steadily at Janine, until at last, unnerved, the younger woman glanced away. She fumbled in her handbag for another cigarette, and her hands shook slightly as she fitted it in the holder. No one moved to light it for her, and her expensive lighter clicking in the silence seemed like a thunderclap in the electric atmosphere. It was she who was the most relieved when Dick Butler entered the room.

He coloured hotly when he saw her, and looked nervously round at the three other motionless people. No one coming into the room at that moment could have failed to sense the tension: it was almost visible.

Janine relaxed and sat down in an armchair. As an actress she knew the value of dominating taller people from a lower level, though as an individual she lacked command.

"Dick came to see me the other night," she began. "After you had left," she added, addressing Geoffrey.

Dick looked thoroughly confused; he blushed to the tips of his ears.

"Here, I say," he muttered, and then, meeting her unrelenting eye, "yes, I did."

"Tell them what you told me," Janine instructed. Her merciless gaze was upon him. Dick cleared his throat.

"I—er—I—" he mumbled, and swallowed.

"Begin at the first night of term," Janine told him. "You saw Mr. Farquhar—" she spoke Peter's name with a sneer, "—where?"

"Coming out of Wilson's dormitory," said Dick reluctantly.

"What time was this?"

"About ten o'clock."

"Now tell them about the bathing incident," Janine pursued inexorably.

"They know about that—everyone knows Wilson funked the water. Mr. Farquhar made an awful fuss about it—made an ass of the boy," said Dick, in a rush of loquacity. He remembered what Peter had said to him then, and his indignation momentarily outran his present fright. "Why, he behaved most unreasonably," he said.

"And then?"

Dick took a deep breath, and then continued unwillingly.

"One night a few weeks ago I heard a noise. It was about eleven o'clock. I looked out of my room and saw Farquhar and Wilson going along the passage," he said.

There was silence.

"Well, have you finished?" It was Marion who spoke.

"Isn't that enough?" demanded Janine. "You'll go to prison for this," she said to Peter, "and the school will be finished."

"Butler, you can go," said Geoffrey shortly. "I'll deal with you later."

Dick hesitated. He glanced at Janine, who merely returned his look with composure.

"Ask Miss Norton to bring Wilson here," Geoffrey ordered.

Marion made a movement of protest, but Geoffrey shook his head at her very slightly. He advanced and stood above Janine, who thereupon got a crick in her neck as she tried to look up at him. She abandoned the attempt, and gazed instead into the grate where the flowers made an audience for her imagination.

"Mrs. Wilson, you have made some unforgivable accusations," he began. "Few schools would contemplate keeping Christopher after what you have said. But I don't think you can be quite yourself. I suggest you apologise to Mr. Farquhar and then go away, and we will forget the whole matter."

"Christopher is leaving," Janine repeated. "And I do not apologise for anything I have said. One does not apologise for the truth."

"You know it isn't true," said Geoffrey. "Wait and see what the boy says himself."

"He'll lie," said Janine.

"He is a truthful boy," said Peter, speaking at last. He could not believe that this scene was really happening. Surely he would wake up in a minute and find himself safely on the games field watching the match?

There was a creaking outside, and Phyllis appeared in the window wheeling Christopher. Peter helped her lift the chair over the threshold and into the room. After the bright sunlight outside it was dark indoors, and for a moment Christopher did not see his mother. Then he recognised her, and turned his head sharply away. Phyllis put a hand on his shoulder.

There was a silence. Janine did not speak to her son, and it was Geoffrey who took the initiative.

"I want you to answer some questions, Wilson," he said gently.

"Yes, sir." Christopher's reply was almost inaudible.

"Do you remember the first night of this term? Did Mr. Farquhar come to your dormitory?"

"Oh, yes." Christopher answered at once. He looked at Peter, but kept his face turned away from his mother. "He gave me a toffee," he said, and then, reddening, put his hand to his mouth. "Oh, sorry, sir. You said not to tell," he said.

"It's all right, Christopher," said Peter. His head was reeling.

Janine was smiling, one eyebrow elevated.

Geoffrey compressed his lips. Then he asked: "Were you ever out of your dormitory at night, when the other boys were asleep?"

Christopher hesitated. He glanced

anxiously at Peter, and then at Phyllis, who nodded.

"Yes," he said at last, lowering his eyes.

"Why?" Geoffrey persisted.

"Tell them, Christopher, it's all right," said Phyllis. It was obvious to her that any concealment was useless.

"It was to fetch some shells. I'd left them on the cliff, and Mr. Farquhar caught me coming back," said Christopher. "He beat me," he added with some pride, for chastisement safely over was sometimes regarded as justifiable ground for boasting.

Peter heard Marion release her breath. Geoffrey never moved.

"I see. Thank you, Wilson," he said. "Just one more thing. You're happy at school, aren't you?"

"Oh yes, sir," Christopher answered at once. "I'm going to be better in time to play football next term, aren't I?"

"You won't be here next term. I'm taking you away," said Janine, at last addressing him.

Now he looked at her.

"Oh, no!" he gasped, and then to Peter, "oh sir, no! Don't let her!" and he bowled his chair forward until he could clutch Peter's sleeve.

"Look at that!" cried Janine. Peter held the boy by the shoulders for a moment.

"It'll be all right, Wilson, don't worry," he said reassuringly. There must be some way out: this could not happen.

"Either he leaves or you do," said Janine, snatching an opportunity of a loophole for herself, for now that she had seen Christopher immobilised in his chair even she was forced to realise his injuries were severe, and she began to think better of undertaking the responsibility for him.

The boy looked in bewilderment at the adult faces. Phyllis's one thought was to remove him from this dreadful scene.

"You won't want Christopher any more just now," she declared, and turned his chair about. As she wheeled him smartly outside Christopher called. "Oh sir, don't make me leave!"

"Don't worry, Christopher," Phyllis said to him. "We won't let you go."

Marion waited until the chair had disappeared from earshot.

"Now you will want to take back your wicked allegations," she told Janine.

280

"I will do no such thing," said Janine. "It's true, and you know it is. Toffees! And you told him not to tell!" She rose to her feet, eyes blazing now as she looked at Peter. "He made all that up about the shells to protect you. You leave, or Christopher does. That's my final word. Dick Butler will swear to what he saw." She picked up her gloves and handbag and prepared to make her exit. "I shall return to London now," she said. "You can have twenty-four hours to decide." With that she went to the door and stood waiting for somebody to open it and release her. It was Marion, not one of the men, who first regained the power of movement and did so. In silence she conducted her to the hall and closed the front door upon her without waiting to see her enter the hired Daimler that waited outside. Then she returned to the drawing-room, where neither of the others had moved an inch or spoken.

"I don't know about you, but I need some fresh air after that," she said with briskness, going to the window and inhaling deeply.

Peter said: "I—I don't know what to say, Geoff."

"Don't try—you don't have to say a word," said Geoffrey at once. "My God, what a devil. I never thought she'd really do it."

"Did you know she was going to?" demanded Peter.

"She made some wild remarks the other day. I thought she'd forget it," said the headmaster. "Marion and I discussed it and we decided not to worry you in case it came to nothing."

"I wish I'd been warned," said Peter bitterly. "Still, I suppose it wouldn't have made much difference. She's got us cold whichever way you look at it."

"There must be a way out," Geoffrey said. "We'll find it."

Peter gave him a grateful look.

"The—the damnable little bitch," said Marion violently, turning to face them. "My goodness, I'd cheerfully push her over the cliff! I never thought she'd do it either, Geoff."

"Of course, we didn't know about Butler," said Geoffrey slowly. "That's a complication, though I think we could deal with him quite easily."

"That stinks," said Marion bluntly.

"Yes," Geoffrey said. "Pretty vile, I agree." He passed his hand over his hair, thoughtfully.

"Of course, she's had it in for you, Peter, because you didn't fall for her too," said Marion. "'Hell hath no fury,' remember. Pity about the toffee. That bit sounds bad."

"Teeth," said Peter briefly. "I meant it as a joke, with matron as the butt." He hunched his shoulder. "That'll teach me to crack jokes. Do you want it in writing, Geoffrey?"

"What?" demanded Geoffrey.

"My resignation, of course," said the younger man.

"Don't be a fool," said Geoffrey. "I'm not losing you for that evil creature."

"You can't let her take the child away," said Peter. "His only hope is to stay here."

"If she does go on with this, no one will believe a word of it," said Geoffrey.

"Mud sticks," Peter replied. "She could ruin the school. We may not think much of her, but she's well known, and people would listen to what she says."

"She'd never take it to Court," said Marion.

"We couldn't risk it," Peter said. "Even without that, a hint of such a thing and Arrowhurst would be done."

"Every mother's nightmare," said Marion slowly. "Mrs. Jones once confided that to me." She turned from the window and smiled at Peter.

"No one who knows you would entertain the idea for a moment," said Geoffrey insistently. "No one would believe it," he repeated.

"You didn't," said Peter, "and I'm grateful. But Marion had a moment's doubt, didn't you, Marion?" He turned to her.

She looked at him. "I didn't doubt you, Peter, don't ever think so. But it was odd about the toffee, and I was glad to hear the child explain about the shells."

"Of course it was odd. It sounds a damned odd story out of context," said Peter. "I found the boy awake and crying, that was why I gave him a toffee."

"Yes, I know, you've done it before with new boys," Marion said.

"What was all that about shells?" asked Geoffrey irritably. He had been walking up and down thinking while the others talked.

"Oh, it's a long story," said Peter. "I didn't worry you about it at the time, but now I see I should have told you." He recounted briefly what had happened.

"Yes, you should have told me," said Geoffrey when he had finished. "But I understand why you didn't. After all, your job is to undertake some of my responsibilities. You acted rightly at the time, and it wouldn't have mattered if this hadn't happened."

"God, I'm sorry, Geoffrey," said Peter wretchedly.

"My dear boy, it isn't your fault," said Geoffrey. "Don't start apologising, for goodness' sake."

"There must be some legal loophole," said Marion. "It can't be possible for such a pack of lies to succeed. The whole thing's the most malicious build-up of coincidences."

"'I have seen the wicked in great power, and spreading himself like a green bay tree,'" quoted Peter with gloom. "Now I know how murderers feel when they get caught on circumstantial evidence."

"Do you remember how that psalm goes on?" asked Marion with a faint smile. "'Yet he passed away, and lo he was not.' Cheer up, you aren't a murderer, and all is not lost yet."

Peter looked at her with surprised respect. Lately Marion had astonished him often, and he knew that he had frequently under-estimated her.

"Butler's the stumbling block," he said, more calmly. "She's obviously got him where she wants him. Besides, I expect he did see me those times."

"No one would believe it," Marion said again.

"You know that a whisper of this outside would finish the school, Marion," said Peter flatly. "Besides, I can't let the child become involved in any more scenes like the one he's just witnessed. She wouldn't hesitate to drag him in to prove her case, and being who she is it would cause a frightful stir."

Marion shrugged and turned away. As she did so a shadow fell across the open french window and a boy appeared.

"Please, sir, Mr. Farquhar," he said, "we're waiting for you on the cricket pitch."

"Oh!" Peter looked blank. He had forgotten the match. "I'm supposed to be umpiring," he said to Geoffrey.

"Oh—all right, go along," said Geoffrey. "We'll talk about it after dinner."

Without another word Peter left them. Geoffrey sank down upon the sofa in an attitude of despair, but Marion squared her shoulders.

"Don't give up, Geoff," she said.

"In twenty years there's never before been even a breath of this," said Geoffrey. "What can we do?"

15

LATER that evening, after dinner, it rained. Steadily it poured down in an endless stream; the air was oppressive, and outside the open windows of the common room the earth blotted up the silently falling water.

"This will swell the peas," said Wilfrid Fitzgibbon with satisfaction, looking out at the garden with a pleased expression on his face. "And the lettuces won't need watering for days." He nodded to himself, and turned back into the room. "Well, what's it going to be tonight?" he asked. "Television or Scrabble? It's no night for outdoor sports."

"There's quite a good play on, I think," said Phyllis, who was sitting on the sofa with a pile of mending; she always undertook the larger part of this chore.

"Oh, don't let's watch the telly," said Ronald. "Surely we can find our own amusement without having it served up to us as to the masses."

"Don't be such a snob, my boy," said Wilfrid. "Look at the horizons that are opened to us by the telly. We can visit the President of the Royal Academy at home, go show jumping with Alan Oliver; and watch rare birds at sunrise, with Peter Scott; all things I, at any rate would be unlikely to do otherwise. Don't scoff at it."

"Yes, but all those dreadful thrillers," protested Ronald.

"Why not? Some of the best brains in the country read thrillers as relaxation," Wilfrid said. "Even bishops have been known to. Besides, the plays aren't always thrillers. Sometimes we can see historical dramas, or romantic comedies, or even Shakespeare."

"How could they?" cried Ronald, shuddering. "Shakespeare!"

"What? Oh, desecrate him, you mean?" asked Wilfrid.

Ronald nodded.

"You think he wrote them then?" said the old man.

"What was he doing, if he wasn't doing that?" said Ronald.

"Quite," said Wilfrid. "I've always

admired the volume of his output. Bacon or Marlowe would have hardly had time to breathe if they'd added it to theirs. But don't you think it's better for the masses, as you so rudely call them, to see a Shakespeare play however bowdlerized, and hear even a tiny part of his wonderful language, than never to see or hear it at all? Perhaps some of them might even be driven to read the original or go to the Old Vic."

"You'll be saying you're in favour of the classics as strip cartoons next," said Ronald with a grin. He and Wilfrid thoroughly enjoyed the arguments which took place between them on every possible occasion and at the least excuse.

"I think I am," said Wilfrid. "Better like that than not to know who Sydney Carton is."

"You can learn history from the *Eagle*," interposed Phyllis. "They've certainly done Nelson on the back."

"We'll be out of a job soon," said Ronald. "It's all too simple. No one will trouble to wade through the real thing, and look what they'll miss."

"It's your task to show 'em," said

Wilfrid. "Well, shall we have a game, or do you want to go and write?"

"I'm stuck," Ronald confessed. "I haven't written a line for weeks."

Wilfrid smiled. "Pity," he said insincerely. "You'll come back to it. Well, who else is going to play? Phyllis?"

"No, not tonight," said Phyllis. "Sorry, but I've got a bit of a headache." She was unable to get her mind away from Janine's visit, and wondered if Geoffrey and Marion were any nearer a solution to the problem as they thrashed it out now in the drawing-room.

"Oh, I'm sorry to hear that," said Wilfrid.

"It's the weather, I expect," said Phyllis. "It's rather thundery."

"Well, I don't know where everyone's got to tonight," said Wilfrid. "They certainly can't be swimming or playing tennis. Butler, how about you? Will you play?"

Dick was sitting with the *Daily Telegraph* up in front of him, hiding from Phyllis.

"No, not tonight, thanks," he said.

"Hm. The weather seems to have got

into everybody," said Wilfrid. "Where's Jenny? Off somewhere with Peter?"

"I've no idea," said Phyllis. "Possibly."

"Oh, well, we'll have to have a duel, Ronald," said the old man, who had lately developed a great passion for Scrabble now that he had found a worthy opponent in Ronald.

They drew for who should start, and Ronald got an A.

"Hm, can't beat that," said Wilfrid, turning up G.

They settled themselves down with a large dictionary on the table, and began to prepare the board and letters.

"Mrs. Wilson came to see the lad this afternoon, I hear," Wilfrid said, arranging his counters on their stand.

"Yes, she did," said Phyllis.

"About time," Ronald said.

Phyllis made no comment.

"Extraordinary female she must be," said Wilfrid. "Eh? What's that, CANAL? That's a dull beginning, Ronald."

"It's the best I can do," said the young man with a smile.

Wilfrid frowned over the board.

"Thanks for the L," he said, arranging

ALIGN around that letter. "I only saw her in chapel that time. Pretty, if you like that delicate, dresden type. Do you, Ronald!"

"What? Oh, good heavens, no," said Ronald. "Phyllis is my ideal woman, didn't you know? I like them tough." He grinned across at Phyllis, who threw a skein of grey wool at him. He tossed it back, and then there was silence while the players brooded over their game.

Z-I-N-K-E, wrote Ronald, around the N of CANAL.

"What has happened to your spelling?" asked Wilfrid. Ronald wore a poker face, and the old man, not to disappoint him, at last said: "I challenge you," and proceeded to look up the word in the dictionary.

"'An old wind instrument—the precursor of the cornet'," he read aloud. "Well, that's yours, Ronald, and I must deduct it. Pity. I suppose you looked it up and had it ready up your sleeve to trick me?"

"I did," said Ronald with a smile. "I had to avenge your 'scazon' the other day."

"You should have known that was

genuine," said Wilfrid. "Shows you haven't had the benefits of a classical education."

"Have you ever heard of a scazon, Phyllis?" asked Ronald.

"No. Should I have?" asked Phyllis. "What is it? One who is scatty?"

"No. It's a curious word, meaning limping—in relation to metre in verse," said Ronald airily. "Or so Wilfrid declares."

"Oh, I see," said Phyllis, to whom the word remained obscure. How nice Ronald was, she reflected. He spent hours talking to Wilfrid and playing the word games the old man enjoyed so much, when he might well prefer to be down on the beach with Judy Palliser, even if he had lost interest in his novel. How unlike Dick. She looked across at the *Daily Telegraph*, which had not moved. Behind it a piece of Dick's carroty hair could just be seen.

"What about you?" said Ronald, writing down his score.

Wilfrid put an E, and an A and an R down on the board to make NEAR "What about me what?" he asked.

"You and Mrs. Wilson. Do you admire

her?" Ronald wanted to know. "Is that all you can do?" he added, with scorn, arranging an L and a Y on the end and making NEARLY with a double score.

"She's a pretty little actress in a fluffy way," said Wilfrid. "I saw her once a long time ago in an amusing play, and thought her decorative; but I prefer Phyllis too."

"Mrs. Wilson has the advantage over me of fewer years," said Phyllis, folding up a pair of socks and sighing because the nametapes had been sewn on in so strange a place that they refused to remain uppermost whatever she did.

"Has she?" asked Wilfrid. "I shouldn't have thought there was much in it."

"I'm flattered," said Phyllis with a smile. She glanced across as the *Telegraph* rustled slightly.

"What about you, Butler? Do you admire Mrs. Wilson, or Janine Dufay, I should say," Wilfrid pursued.

Dick threw down the paper, got to his feet and rushed from the room.

The other two men looked after him in amazement. Phyllis found that her heart was thumping hard.

"Dear me," said Wilfrid mildly, peering

at the growing crossword in front of him. "Our young friend is in a bad mood tonight."

"He's a bit smitten with Mrs. W.," said Ronald. "He rather fell for her after seeing that play she was in."

"Ah, I see. I was tactless. Well, well, he'll get over it, no doubt," said Wilfred. "That was yesterday's paper he was so earnestly reading, I hope he found it instructive. Now, come, Ronald. We aren't attending to the game." He frowned, squinting at the board. Phyllis longed to tell them both what had passed that afternoon. Like Dick, she suddenly felt unable to be still, and began to put away her work.

"Oh—off, Phyl?" asked Wilfrid, as she rose.

"Yes. I've one or two things to see to in the office," she said. "Then for an early night. Goodnight, both of you."

"Goodnight, Phyllis," they both said, and she went out of the room. She put the mended socks away in the boys' clothes' lockers, and then she went on downstairs to the drawing-room.

It was nearly dark now outside, and the

room was hazy with cigarette smoke. Marion and Geoffrey sat in attitudes of dejection on either side of the fireplace, by the light of one tall standard lamp. Peter, whom she had expected to find with them, was nowhere to be seen.

"I wondered if you'd thought of anything," said Phyllis. She suddenly felt herself an intruder upon their solitude, a feeling she had never had before in all the years that she had worked for Geoffrey.

"Oh, come in, Phyl," said Geoffrey. "Sit down. No, we haven't found a way out, but Peter has vanished, saying he insists on resigning."

"He went through there," said Marion, waving at the window.

"Is he all right? It's pouring with rain," said Phyllis.

"He isn't out of his mind, if that's what you mean," said Geoffrey. "He's just in despair. Do him good to walk about a bit."

"I suppose so," said Phyllis. She sat down on the sofa. "There must be a solution," she said. "Peter can't possibly go."

"No, of course he can't," said Geoffrey.

"But that woman could make a lot of trouble for us."

"It's all my fault. I sent Dick Butler round to see her when we went to the theatre," said Phyllis. "I thought it would be a joke and do him good, and now look where it's landed us."

"For goodness' sake don't let's start allocating the blame," said Marion. "That won't get us anywhere. We're all responsible. Dick's no more than a child himself."

"How could she? A boy that age," exclaimed Phyllis with a shiver.

"He made her feel young again herself, I expect," said Marion shortly. "It's happened before. But I doubt if it was roses all the way for him."

"I expect he felt himself a hell of a fellow," said Geoffrey.

"I think he's terrified," said Marion. "He won't forget this afternoon in a hurry."

"Worrying about Butler won't help us decide on a plan of action," said Geoffrey. He passed his hand over his hair and looked at Marion.

"We needn't count him as a menace,"

she said. "We can easily third degree him and get him to retract. If it came to the point Mrs. Wilson could never make a case against Peter. No reputable lawyer would touch it. She must have a considerable reputation of her own; any woman who behaves with men as we've seen her doing must, and particularly if she's already well-known. But she could cause a lot of nasty gossip and make a scandal, simply because she *is* well-known. I think our best idea is to try and play for time. When she thinks things over she'll realise that the boy will be a liability for months, and she won't want to find herself landed with looking after him. She'll learn that it isn't easy, however famous she is, to get him into another school, and she may think better of it. After all, she came here today intent on taking him away at once, and she left without him, so that's one round to us."

She walked up and down the room, whistling under her breath, perfectly dressed and with not a hair out of place on her shining auburn head. Phyllis looked at her with new eyes. It was Marion, now, who had taken charge of the situation. She herself sat in a corner of the sofa trying to ignore her headache; and Geoffrey, slumped in his chair, looking exhausted and defeated. But Marion's eyes flashed with courage, and she strode up and down with purposeful steps.

"If we can spin things out for a few days she might be in a better frame of mind, and we could try and talk her round," she said, thinking aloud. "Of course we'd have to do it in some way that saved her face."

"Well, we'll try it," said Geoffrey. "It's the only idea we've got so far. How can we do it?"

"We'll tell her the boy isn't fit to be moved yet," said Marion. "We must get Alec Hunt to back us up—you get hold of him in the morning, Phyllis, and fix him. It shouldn't be difficult. Even a few days will help, and she may start to change her mind. It will give us time to think up a way of making it look like her own idea and not a climb-down."

"All right, I'll get on to Alec in the morning," said Phyllis. "I'm sorry, Geoffrey," she said again.

"Oh—" he brushed aside her words. "I ought never to have engaged that boy—I ought to have spotted he was no good," he said irritably.

"It wasn't altogether Dick's fault," said Marion. "Neither you nor Peter, with all your years, could cope with Janine. How could a boy of eighteen, with no experience, stand a chance when she made up her mind?"

Phyllis looked wretched. "I knew what she was like. We three all did. Jenny thought he ought not to be left alone with her, and I just laughed because I was annoyed with him."

"Phyllis, you're much too nice to know just what Janine's like," said Marion. "But I'm not, and I do know. However, I didn't realise what far-reaching harm can come from such an escapade. Probably in the end young Dick will grow up to be a wiser and a better man. Don't blame yourself too much. And now I think we'd better all get to bed, you two look like a couple of wrecks. Come along."

She began to plump up the cushions on the chairs, and Phyllis automatically crossed to close the french window

"What about Peter?" she asked.

"He's probably come in another way,"

said Geoffrey. "Anyway he'll go round if he finds this is locked."

"All right." She turned the key with a click, and as she did so the door burst open. Ronald Cross, ashen-faced stood revealed.

"Phyllis—sir! Come quickly," he gasped. "There's been an accident."

That afternoon, after leaving the drawing-room, Christopher had been wheeled back to the cricket pitch to watch the end of the match. He felt sick with fright. Miss Norton had promised he would not be taken away from Arrowhurst, but if his mother meant it how could they prevent her from carrying out her intention? Someone had to pay for him, he knew: if he wasn't paid for he couldn't stay. His mother had said that either he or Mr. Farquhar must leave. Christopher did not worry about the strangeness of these clauses: grown-ups, and particularly his mother, often made demands that appeared to be quite without reason or logic. He realised, irrevocably, that his mother hated him, otherwise she would not do this to him. With adult acceptance he no longer cared. Instead, he resolved, single-mindedly, to make it impossible for her to carry out her threat. Mr. Cross had jokingly warned him not to break his plasters: that was what he must now do.

Christopher tried to make the wheelchair run away, down the hill, as he came back to the school buildings from the playing fields, but Mr. Cross caught him as it gathered speed and kept a restraining hand on the back of it for the rest of the way.

After tea, he wheeled himself down the passage and into the workshop where the boys did carpentry and handwork. He travelled between the benches that were covered with half-finished cane-sided trays, tall thin bookshelves and weirdly shaped boxes, to the tool cupboard, and removed a hammer which he smuggled up to bed with him, tucked under his jersey; but matron found it and took it away, muttering crossly.

Later, Christopher lay in bed waiting till all was quiet. One by one the sounds in the big building diminished and ceased. Matron went away downstairs for her supper, and presently he heard her sturdy feet flat-footedly returning along the passage to her sitting-room. Doors opened and shut below: every sound was carried clearly to the sharp ears of the waiting boy. He heard the swish of the rain as it began to fall outside. Someone in the distance was playing the piano, something by Schumann that he recognised. Only Miss Wayne, here, could play like that. He listened with pleasure for quite a time, and then she stopped too.

Christopher sat up. He heaved his two plastered legs over the edge of the bed and beat at the casts with his wooden-backed hairbrush, but it made not the slightest imprint. Somehow he got himself right out of bed. He could not stand alone, so he let himself fall to the floor and slid along on his pyjama seat over to the door. He turned the handle and opened it, spinning himself out of the way without difficulty on the highly-polished brown lino. He navigated himself out, and on down the passage to the top of the stairs. He looked down the steep flight, and almost turned back: then he thought again of his mother. Christopher drew a deep breath; clutching the banister post he dragged himself upright until he was standing at the head of the stairs. He swayed a little. Then he put a foot forward, closed his eyes, and let go with his hands. Loss of balance did the rest and he fell headlong down to the landing below.

It was easy now to play for time. Even Janine was forced to accept an indefinite truce. Christopher lay in Charnton hospital once again, with a fresh bandage round his head and new plasters on his legs. Apart from bruises and shock he had not added to his injuries; even his mending ribs were made no worse. He lay silently in his narrow bed, remote and withdrawn, waiting, like everyone else, for the next development; and had they but known it, fully determined to continue smashing his plasters every time crisis loomed. He had no idea that he might have killed himself, hurtling down the steep staircase.

Exams had begun. Phyllis was busy typing out stencils for the papers, with questions so difficult that she knew she would find herself at the bottom of Form II if required to give the future tense of "amo" or write a potted biography of

Edward the Confessor. A few kind people like Peter and Ronald typed their own papers, and Wilfrid rolled the copies off the duplicator. It was a busy time, as she had also to begin making end-of-term arrangements. There were passports to check for the boys who would fly overseas to join their parents abroad. Some boys going to Africa and the Far East had to have injections against various diseases: documents flew back and forth, and Alec Hunt, the school doctor, was in and out with his needles and pen, pricking and signing. Matron, when the new clothes lists came from the printers, suddenly decided that the four pairs of grey stockings which had been adequate for ten years were no longer enough, with things as they were at the laundry; and had to be pacified and have her mind changed so that Phyllis need not write alterations on all the lists. Mrs. Sparrow wrote to ask was an overcoat really necessary for Sparrow II who was coming next term, as in two winters his elder brother had never yet worn his. Another new boy's mother decided that after all she could not bear to part with her infant, and his vacancy had to be offered to the next name on the crowded waiting list.

Jennifer had little to do. Her music curriculum was upset by exams, and she had few classes. She spent much of her time helping Phyllis wade through the pile of routine work, addressing envelopes, entering up the extras on the accounts and stamping up staff insurance cards.

"What is the matter with Peter, Phyllis?" she asked at last, two days after Christopher's fall, as they sat together in the office. Phyllis was working out how much PAYE to deduct from the domestic staff's wage packets, and Jennifer was writing out cheques and entering items in the large ledger to pay the enormous housekeeping bills.

Phyllis counted on her fingers and quickly wrote a figure on the card before her. Then she looked enquiringly at Jennifer.

"He looks awful, and he won't say what it is, and he'll hardly talk to me," said the girl. "What have I done?"

"It isn't you," said Phyllis. "There's a crisis."

"I thought there must be something. He

keeps being closeted with the headmaster, and they both look about ninety all of a sudden?" said Jennifer. "Is it to do with Christopher Wilson? His falling down the stairs can't have been an accident."

"It wasn't," said Phyllis briefly. "He wanted to make quite sure that he wouldn't be in a condition to be removed by his mother."

Jennifer was astounded. She stared at Phyllis, who said, "You've a right to know what's going on, because Peter is heavily involved. I shall tell you." She proceeded to do so, and the girl listened to her in increasing dismay and horror.

"But it's quite impossible!" she cried.

"Yes, of course it is," Phyllis agreed, "but outsiders don't know Peter like we do, and when a well-known actress starts that sort of rumour some people will believe her."

"But surely she could be had up for defamation of character, or something?" cried Jennifer.

"I expect so, but it would all be very sordid, and however successfully Peter fought her in public some people wouldn't be convinced. He thinks the school would

308

be ruined for ever, and he doesn't want more harm to come to the boy, which would happen if he was dragged into it."

"But she can't get away with it!" Jennifer said.

"Marion thinks she'll get sick of the idea if we can just hang on for a bit," said Phyllis. "She thinks it will all die down. I don't see it myself—I think it'll be like a smouldering bonfire ready to burst into sparks at any moment, but she's convinced Geoffrey, and I certainly can't think of any other solution."

"Oh, poor Peter! How dreadful for him," said Jennifer.

"Yes, it is," said Phyllis.

"Why wouldn't he tell me?"

"How could he, Jenny? You couldn't expect him to."

"But he'd know—he couldn't imagine I'd believe it, surely?' cried Jennifer.

"He might. He's nearly out of his mind with the whole business. He can't see straight about it at all," said Phyllis.

"I don't see how anyone can," said Jennifer miserably.

But Marion could. She was at that moment

in the drawing-room confronting Peter and Geoffrey.

"Give me a good reference, Geoffrey, and I'll get a job somewhere in the north," Peter had just said, with a gesture in the direction of jocularity.

"If you insist on adopting this attitude, Peter, you'll make yourself look guilty," said Marion sternly. "Pull yourself together, for goodness' sake. I'm quite sure not a single parent would believe a word that woman said."

"Oh, yes, they would," said Peter dully. He did feel guilty: he had allowed Christopher to mean more to him than the rest of the boys; he had given much more thought and attention to him; the fact that Christopher needed more than most of the others was something he had forgotten.

"God, how obstinate you are!" cried Marion. "I could slap you, Peter. Look at you, so smug, determined to be a martyr. Think of what all this means to Geoffrey and me! Who's going to take this place on after us if you don't? We can't let a woman like that ruin all that we've achieved with her nonsense. You owe more than that to Geoffrey—isn't he to have the benefit of your service now, when it's at last of value, after all the years he's spent teaching you to follow after him?"

Peter put a hand to his head, which ached with weariness. He had scarcely slept since Mrs. Wilson's visit; he did not know which way to turn or where his duty lay.

"You make me sound ungrateful. I'm not—you know I can't bear to think of leaving, but it's the only thing to do," he said. "If you can find another way out, Marion, then let's take it."

Geoffrey got up and crossed over to the fireplace.

"Let's leave it a bit longer, Peter," he said. "Nothing much can happen while the child is in hospital. You get Phyllis to give you something to make you sleep tonight. Then, when you aren't quite so tired, we'll discuss it again. We'll never get anywhere like this."

Peter shrugged. "Very well, Geoffrey, if you say so," he said. "But my mind's made up. I can't see any other course to take."

"You aren't on duty till after break, are you?" said Marion. "Why don't you find

Jennifer and take her for a swim. It's a lovely day and it would do you both good. She's helping Phyllis in the office."

"How can I even talk to Jenny with all this hanging over me?" demanded Peter.

"Oh, do stop behaving like Hamlet," cried Marion in exasperation. "The poor girl is worried stiff about you—you're making her thoroughly miserable. You're going to marry her, aren't you?"

"Not now," said Peter. "How can I ask her now?"

"If you want something in this world, Peter, you've got to go out and get it," said Marion ruthlessly. "You can't expect it to fall into your lap without some effort on your part. The Lord helps those who help themselves. My advice to you is to stop dramatising yourself and at least go and talk to her. Let her, anyway, have a chance to decide."

Peter looked at her uncertainly. He wanted to be convinced, but still was not quite. Marion stood, eyes blazing with passion, looking perfectly splendid. Neither of the men had ever before seen her so roused.

Thus they were, the three of them,

when the door opened and a tall man with dark hair and a red round face walked into the room. "I'm sorry—I wouldn't let the maid announce me, I just walked right in," he said, addressing Marion. "I'm John Wilson."

16

MARION did not lose her composure for an instant. "You've been wonderfully quick," she said. "Thank goodness. This is my husband, and Peter Farquhar, our senior master."

Mr. Wilson shook hands with the other two men, who were still stunned by his sudden eruption into the room. They recovered, however, enough to find cigarettes and a chair to offer their unexpected visitor, but it was Marion who handled the conversation that followed.

Later, she explained.

"It was such a fantastic situation! Here we all were, being held at pistol point by a wicked and unscrupulous woman, about to sacrifice either Peter or Christopher, one or the other, at her decree. I couldn't let it happen without raising a finger. At first I thought of getting on to the aunt in Cumberland, but we knew she was hard up, and a vicar's wife, with a lot of children of her own. Christopher seems to me to need a lot of love, so I thought I'd try his father first. Do you remember what we were saying the other day, about the custody of the child? As he'd been living with his paternal grandmother for most of his life I began to wonder if we'd got that right.

"I rang up Mr. Wilson, in America. I knew none of you would let me do it if I asked you, you'd go on saying we mustn't interfere, so I did it in the middle of the night, after the second accident. I explained what had been happening all this term, and he said he would come as soon as he could get on a plane. I knew then that everything would be all right, but I didn't think he would get here so soon; that was why I was trying to play for time. Mr. Wilson told me on the telephone that he had got the custody of Christopher; it seems he divorced her, not the other way round as we'd been so lightly assuming. Knowing her, I can't think why we were so dense. But as you heard him say just now, he thought the child might need his mother, and he wanted him to have an English upbringing, so when he was sent by his firm to America he decided to agree to Mrs. Wilson having "care and control" of the boy, as it's legally called, I believe; and to keep out of his life himself, so that he wouldn't be submitted to that awful pull in two directions that we've seen before."

It was after lunch. Mr. Wilson had set off for London, to interview his former wife, a task no one envied him. Marion, Geoffrey, Peter and Phyllis were sitting in the garden amid the debris of their coffee. Overhead, the sun shone, and in the school Rest was in progress. Form I lay on their beds with *The Swift* or books, while their elders were read aloud to by the masters on duty, *Treasure Island* in the library, and *Ivanhoe* in the big school-room.

"How did you find his address?" asked the practical Phyllis, who knew it was not among her records.

"I rang up the bank," said Sherlock Marion, not without pride. "They looked up how the fees were paid, and then got on to Mrs. Wilson's bank in London, who supplied the name of the American bank who pay her allowance. She doesn't have alimony, of course, just money for Christopher. It was rather complicated finding it all out, and very decent of the banks. I don't think they're meant to disclose that sort of information, but I said it was life or death."

"It might well have been," said Geoffrey grimly.

"I shudder to think what the telephone bill will be like," said Marion with a smile. "I don't think Charnton exchange has ever had so much excitement."

"Do you think Mr. Wilson was right not to go and see Christopher before he went to London?" asked Phylllis. "We don't know what the child's been told about him. He may expect somebody awful, and he hasn't seen him since he was a baby. I thought he was a dear."

"Yes, so did I," said Marion. "Somehow I don't think young Christopher will pay very much attention now to anything his mother may have said. She's already shown him how worthless her promises are."

"Do you think she'll let his father have the boy?" asked Peter.

"I don't suppose she'll make it easy for

him," said Geoffrey, "but she obviously finds the child a handicap to her *modus vivendi*."

"I wonder why she bothered about the 'care and control,'" said Phyllis. "She's not in the least maternal."

"Vindictiveness makes people do queer things," said Marion, "and the law is very odd too. It thinks a mother should have a hand in her children's upbringing, however bad a hat she is."

"What a strange judge it must have been who thought Mrs. Wilson should," said Peter.

"She probably wasn't nearly as bad then as she is now," said Marion. "I think up to a point the reasoning is right, but theories often break down in practice. If Mrs. Jones, for instance, threw her bonnet over the windmill, I would be the first to say she should have custody, care, and control."

Everyone laughed at the improbability of this event.

"Well, I back Mr. Wilson to succeed," said Marion. "If he can't persuade her today, he'll obviously go to court, where we will support him." She looked at her hearers. "Yes, Geoffrey, we will," she emphasised. "You can't sit on fences always. But Mr. Wilson looks to me like a pretty successful sort of man. I think he'll deal with her."

"I agree," said Geoffrey. He still felt events rushing past too fast for him to comprehend. He looked at Marion: she was sitting in one of the new canvas chairs with aluminium frames that she had bought this term after laddering her stockings on the old wooden ones. She sat upright, a hand on either arm; the full skirt of her blue dress covered the bright red canvas; and her long, slim legs, in the sheerest stockings, were crossed at the ankle. (No one had ever seen Marion bare-legged, except on the beach.) Her face was composed, smiling a little because she felt pleased with herself, and her lovely hair framed its perfect oval with shining waves, brushed back to show her delicate ears. Her long neck made a graceful curve as it disappeared into the simple shirt-like top of her dress; she wore a white necklace of coral that Geoffrey had given her, years ago. She had seldom worn it: he thought she did not care for it, and was strangely glad as he recognised it now about her neck.

She looked at him calmly and smiled. Geoffrey felt that he was seeing her for the first time. Phyllis watched them both as they gazed steadily at each other, and then she got up abruptly to begin gathering up the coffee cups.

"I must fly—I've left chaos in the office," she said, a little incoherently, and clattered away down the flagged path, frightening a thrush who was cracking snail shells loudly on it.

"Peter, now will you take Jenny for a swim?" said Marion.

Peter had risen to help with the cups. He looked from one to the other of his employers, and the haggard expression dropped away from his face.

"Yes, go and find her, Peter," said Geoffrey. "Hurry up."

Peter hesitated; then his cheerful grin, that had not been seen for several days, appeared. He strode rapidly away, his long legs making criss-cross shadows on the grass.

Geoffrey got up and went over to his wife. She put a hand out, and he clasped it gently. It was so long since he had courted her with words that now he could not suddenly begin. Watching his face, Marion understood. She felt tears at the back of her eyes as she knew that never in their lives would they be closer to one another than at this moment.

"Dear Geoffrey, are you pleased with me?" she said.

Mr. Wilson returned on the evening train, weary but triumphant. He did not reveal how his victory had been won; Geoffrey guessed money had played a large part in the argument.

"I shall get it all tied up legally, of course," said Mr. Wilson. "But there's plenty of time to see about that—I called my lawyer this evening."

He looked a very bluff and British man, but his speech contained a few colloquial Americanisms that made obvious where he dwelt.

Marion suggested a bath, and Geoffrey a large whisky and soda; Mr. Wilson was to stay at Arrowhurst for the present. He was a pleasant guest. Instead of dining, that night, with the rest of the staff, Marion had arranged that she and

Geoffrey, with Peter, should dine alone with their visitor. She liked eleventh hour challenges, and had achieved an impressive menu with avocado pears, lobster in rich sauce, and a fluffy chocolate pudding. Geoffrey produced some excellent hock, and the company enjoyed an elegant evening, even though the cook had earlier been plunged into dismay at having to concoct it. During the meal Mr. Wilson entertained his hosts with an amusing description of his efforts to secure an immediate flight passage, and then of his impressions of London, where he had not been for seven years.

After dinner they went, with their coffee and liqueurs, into the garden, and Phyllis, by invitation, joined them.

"And now, Mrs. Frost," said Mr. Wilson, setting down his glass. "What sort of a boy is my son?"

It was Peter who, the next morning, took Mr. Wilson to the hospital. No one knew what sort of mental image Christopher had of his unknown father, and it had been decided that he should simply be told that his father had come all the way from

America to see him because he had heard about his accident. Christopher had still not been told about his grandmother's death, but it was hoped that this hurdle could be postponed until the more imminent one had been negotiated.

Mr. Wilson confided, as Peter abandoned him in the corridor outside Christopher's ward, that he felt as nervous as a cat, but he looked so extremely kind and genial that the younger man did not have a moment's doubt about the successful outcome of the meeting.

He hurried in to prepare Christopher. "He's awfully nice, you'll like him," Peter ended. "I'll get him now."

Christopher had only a moment in which to be scared before he saw a very large man with a very big smile coming down the ward to his corner. Mr. Wilson had, in the past, batted for his county, landed by parachute at Arnhem, and escaped three times from German prison camps, but he had never before in his forty years been quite so afraid of facing anything as he was of the unknown little boy in the corner bed who watched his advance with unblinking large brown eyes, exactly like his own.

They looked at each other for a moment, Christopher staring, his father racking his brains for what to say.

"Well, Chris," he said at length. "Can I sit down? I've come over two thousand miles to see you."

"Is that true?" asked Christopher. "Really and truly?" The voice was thin: he's very weak, thought the man.

"Yes, it is," he said calmly. "Really and truly. I thought you might be short of something to read. Let's look what's here, shall we?" He produced a parcel from under his arm, and somehow, in the commotion that followed, of undoing the string and inspecting the books it contained, everything came all right.

When Peter returned some time later Mr. Wilson was sitting by the bed reading an adventure of Roy Rogers aloud as if he had been accustomed to reading to his son every day for the past nine years, and Christopher was lying with his hands folded over the pile of Biggles books and sports annuals that lay on his chest.

Mr. Wilson knew that schoolboys

thought kissing was weedy, girly stuff, and very soppy; but all the same, when he rose to leave, he risked it, and was rewarded by a hug of bear-like ferocity from a pair of very skinny arms.

Phyllis and Geoffrey were finishing the reports. Term had ended; ninety-nine of the Arrowhurst boys were already scattered to their homes; the hundredth, Christopher, had gone today. The ultimate future was uncertain, but he was flying out to America with his father tonight, and would return next term. Later it would be decided whether he would remain on or enrol at an American school. Mr. Wilson himself, reluctant to abandon his plans for an English education for his son, was full of ideas for seeking a transfer to a European department of the large oil concern in which he was now a high executive, but he had re-married some years ago, and a talk with his wife was necessary first.

She had written many times to Christopher, and sent snapshots of the large white house where they lived with two dogs and a cat. Mr. Wilson had told

Marion that she was thrilled at the idea of having Christopher; she had often before suggested that he should see the child, but he had rigidly adhered to his intention not to become a distraction in the boy's life. Even he, disillusioned as he was, had been astounded by his meeting with Janine, and was bitterly regretting that Christopher had been left with her so long.

"Look at this," said Geoffrey, holding up a sheet of paper on which he was about to write his own report. "' His attention wanders with the ease of thistledown in a high wind.' Ronald's words, those are. Poor Sparrow, so does mine." He wrote some cheering sentences in the empty space; Sparrow was a nice little boy who never struck the first blow in a fight. "Here's another: 'Drastic measures are necessary if he is to grasp even the most simple rules of mathematics.' That's Jones II. It's up to Ronald to apply the drastic measures needed. I wonder how long it will take him to give up getting his revenge on his own teachers by these flights of fancy. 'Could do better if he tried' is quite enough." He signed his name on Jones II's report and took an envelope, ready addressed, from the pile on his desk.

Phyllis had not been listening.

"I'm leaving, Geoffrey," she said.

He was looking at another report, and did not understand her words at first. Then the meaning of them penetrated and he swung round to look at her.

"Phyllis! You don't mean that," he said. "Not after all this time!"

"I do mean it," she said, keeping her voice steady. "I—I've been screwing myself up for days to tell you, it's—it isn't easy."

"No." He stared at her. "I don't suppose it is."

She rushed on: "You don't need me, so don't start pretending you can't manage without me. Marion is quite wonderful, as you very well know, and while you've got her you'll be able to cope with anything from mad parents to government inspectors. Any typist from Charnton can deal with what she hasn't time for."

"But why, Phyllis?" Geoffrey asked. "What will you do? Why must you go?"

"I've got too big for my boots," she said, trying to sound cheerful. But her face was grave as she continued: "It was I who persuaded Peter not to tell you about Christopher Wilson's midnight adventure. It was I who indirectly caused Dick Butler to take up with that harpy. I nearly lost you everything, Geoffrey."

"Oh, Phyllis, don't be ridiculous," said Geoffrey. "If we all went about looking for cause and effect like that we'd never have a moment's peace of mind."

"I was getting a power complex," Phyllis insisted. "Or an infallibility one, whichever you prefer. I thought this place would collapse without me, but it won't, and I'm going to prove that I can manage without you." She hesitated, while he still regarded her in stupefaction. Then, very deliberately, she said: "I'm going to marry Alec Hunt."

"Phyllis!" Too late Geoffrey realised that his startled exclamation was hardly flattering.

Phyllis did not miss the note in his voice. She looked down at her hands, and plodded on: "We'll be living near Manchester. He's going to specialise at last, with children. You know how good he's always been with the boys, and this is something he's wanted to do for years. He's been offered a splendid opening up there." She paused. "He's proposed to me before," she said defiantly.

"Oh, Phyl, my dear, I'm so glad," said Geoffrey, still stunned, but recovering. He got up. "He's a good chap, and a lucky fellow to get you. I hope you'll be very happy."

He crossed to where she sat at the side of the desk, bent down, and kissed her chastely on the forehead. Phyllis blinked; he smelt faintly of tweed and expensive hair oil. But she would not weaken. Geoffrey did not need her, he had not needed her for years, though she had flattered herself that she was indispensable. She had no more doubts about that now; Arrowhurst would thrive without her, her role here had become a negative one. Ahead lay something positive, frightening, but worthwhile. She did not yet love Alec, but from the abiding friendship and respect between them she was sure something more would grow.

She got up.

"Marion will be back from the station soon," she said. "I'm going to pack."

Christopher sat bolt upright in the train. His legs were still in plaster, stretched out along the seat, but he could walk a little. His father had lifted him into the train. It was lucky he was so big and strong, for he would have to do a lot of carrying at the airport.

The train moved off.

"Have a toffee, Chris?" said Mr. Wilson, holding out a bag.

"Thanks," said Christopher, and added: "Daddy."

They sucked in companionable silence for a while, and watched the summer countryside flash past. Then the two dark heads turned, and the two pairs of large brown eyes looked at one another.

Christopher parked his toffee in his cheek.

"Shall we see real cowboys in America?" he asked.

We hope this Large Print edition gives you the pleasure and enjoyment we ourselves experienced in its publication.

There are now more than 1,600 titles available in this ULVERSCROFT Large Print Series. Ask to see a Selection at your nearest library.

The Publisher will be delighted to send you, free of charge, upon request a complete and up-to-date list of all titles available.

Ulverscroft Large Print Books Ltd.
The Green, Bradgate Road
Anstey
Leicestershire
England

GUIDE
TO THE COLOUR CODING
OF
ULVERSCROFT BOOKS

Many of our readers have written to us expressing their appreciation for the way in which our colour coding has assisted them in selecting the Ulverscroft books of their choice. To remind everyone of our colour coding— this is as follows:

BLACK COVERS
Mysteries

★

BLUE COVERS
Romances

★

RED COVERS
Adventure Suspense and General Fiction

★

ORANGE COVERS
Westerns

★

GREEN COVERS
Non-Fiction

MYSTERY TITLES
in the
Ulverscroft Large Print Series

Henrietta Who?	*Catherine Aird*
Slight Mourning	*Catherine Aird*
The China Governess	*Margery Allingham*
Coroner's Pidgin	*Margery Allingham*
Crime at Black Dudley	*Margery Allingham*
Look to the Lady	*Margery Allingham*
More Work for the Undertaker	
	Margery Allingham
Death in the Channel	*J. R. L. Anderson*
Death in the City	*J. R. L. Anderson*
Death on the Rocks	*J. R. L. Anderson*
A Sprig of Sea Lavender	*J. R. L. Anderson*
Death of a Poison-Tongue	*Josephine Bell*
Murder Adrift	*George Bellairs*
Strangers Among the Dead	*George Bellairs*
The Case of the Abominable Snowman	
	Nicholas Blake
The Widow's Cruise	*Nicholas Blake*
The Brides of Friedberg	*Gwendoline Butler*
Murder By Proxy	*Harry Carmichael*
Post Mortem	*Harry Carmichael*
Suicide Clause	*Harry Carmichael*
After the Funeral	*Agatha Christie*
The Body in the Library	*Agatha Christie*

FICTION TITLES
in the
Ulverscroft Large Print Series

ROMANCE TITLES
in the
Ulverscroft Large Print Series

The Smile of the Stranger	*Joan Aiken*
Busman's Holiday	*Lucilla Andrews*
Flowers From the Doctor	*Lucilla Andrews*
Nurse Errant	*Lucilla Andrews*
Silent Song	*Lucilla Andrews*
Merlin's Keep	*Madeleine Brent*
Tregaron's Daughter	*Madeleine Brent*
The Bend in the River	*Iris Bromige*
A Haunted Landscape	*Iris Bromige*
Laurian Vale	*Iris Bromige*
A Magic Place	*Iris Bromige*
The Quiet Hills	*Iris Bromige*
Rosevean	*Iris Bromige*
The Young Romantic	*Iris Bromige*
Lament for a Lost Lover	*Philippa Carr*
The Lion Triumphant	*Philippa Carr*
The Miracle at St. Bruno's	*Philippa Carr*
The Witch From the Sea	*Philippa Carr*
Isle of Pomegranates	*Iris Danbury*
For I Have Lived Today	*Alice Dwyer-Joyce*
The Gingerbread House	*Alice Dwyer-Joyce*
The Strolling Players	*Alice Dwyer-Joyce*
Afternoon for Lizards	*Dorothy Eden*
The Marriage Chest	*Dorothy Eden*